NOTHiNG SERIOUS

DANIEL KLEIN
NOTHiNG
SERIOUS

a novel

THE PERMANENT PRESS
Sag Harbor, NY 11963

For information, address:
  The Permanent Press
  4170 Noyac Road
  Sag Harbor, NY 11963
  www.thepermanentpress.com

Library of Congress Cataloging-in-Publication Data

  Klein, Daniel M.—
    Nothing serious : a novel / Daniel Klein.
      pages cm
    ISBN 978-1-57962-314-2
      1. Philosophy—Fiction. 2. Periodicals—Publishing—Fiction.
    I. Title.

  PS3561.L344N68 2013
  813'.54—dc23   2012048038

Printed in the United States of America

For the late and dearly missed

Jack Nessel

ACKNOWLEDGMENTS

A number of my friends have generously read various drafts of this little opus and I want them to know how much I appreciate their comments, even though, occasionally, these comments forced me to consider another line of work—say, night clerk at my local convenience store.

In particular, I am grateful to Bridget Potter, who suggested a major shift in the way I told the story. I am also indebted to Peter Cherneff, Craig Lambert, Pat Bonavitacola, Samara Klein, Freke Vuijst, and Tom Cathcart.

My agent, Julia Lord, and my publishers, Martin and Judith Shepard at The Permanent Press, are, as always, way too good to me.

Also, a tip of my philosophical hat to Professor Tim Madigan whose review of Tom's and my book *Plato and a Platypus Walk into a Bar* in *Philosophy Now* magazine got me to thinking about what a relevant philosophy magazine might possibly be.

—DMK

"**Philosophy**, *n.* A route of many roads leading
from nowhere to nothing."

—AMBROSE BIERCE
The Devil's Dictionary

Bobbing around inside Digby Maxwell's estimable bag of mental tricks is his uncanny ability to see himself objectively—quite literally, as an object. With an almost negligible neuronal nudge, he can leap into the very opposite of a solipsistic universe, one without an 'I' anywhere to be found, but nonetheless a universe that contains this fellow Digby Maxwell.

Digby considers this trick of his to be a singular talent, in fact the fount of his success, such as it is—or, at least, such as it was. But other people, like, say, his former wife, Fanny, see it as just one more example of his lack of a genuine personal identity. "Underneath all that devil-may-care charm and self-deprecating wit," she says, "there's just no 'there' there." And, of course, philosophically speaking, the Cartesians on campus would insist that there has to be an 'I' who perceives this objective Digby: Cogito Ergo, etcetera.

Not so, claims Maxwell. In mid-trick, thoughts about himself—or about anything else, for that matter—are attached to nothing at all. To no I, no me, no ego. The thoughts are just floating out there in the ether.

Now where was I?

Digby Maxwell is posed in front of a blazing fireplace in the heavily draped salon of a Victorian mansion, a glass of English sherry in his hand. He is wearing a frayed tweed jacket with leather-cloaked buttons that he purchased just two days ago in an upscale used clothing shop in Greenwich Village. For this occasion, he has also donned a knowing, mildly supercilious smile, but it, like his ability to focus on the people around him, is rapidly fading. The reason for this is that he is just a few tokes short of being seriously stoned; and the reason for that is that he is trying desperately to medicate his panic.

So far, his strategy of confining most of his conversation to inside his head is working smoothly. He has met and hand-shaked all the key players in this bead game of which he is the newly recruited captain, and he has done so without uttering more than two or three words to each shakee.

But now he sees that his hostess, Felicia Hastings, is look-ing at him expectantly. His guess is that she desires a *bon mot* to drop from his twitchy lips fairly soon now. Although the widow Hastings is clearly over-endowed with self-confidence, she nonetheless would appreciate some public sign—just a clue, really—that Digby, her new employee, is not a total chuckle-head. It is already common knowledge on campus and in the offices of *Cogito* magazine that not only is he lacking *any* advanced academic degree—let alone one in philosophy—but his editorial experience is limited to the subject of what is charitably known as 'popular culture.' It was precisely for this expertise that Ms. Hastings selected Digby to become the new editor-in-chief of *Cogito*; but, alas, it is also why she now is all but poking him with her rheumatoid fingers to induce him to say something witty or at least something New Yorky to bolster her counterintuitive selection.

"There's something about a Victorian home that makes me want to commit an act of gross indecency," he says, his medication bearing some of the responsibility for his choice of words.

Ms. Hastings trills a little laugh, but the guests on either side of her, June MacLane and Elliot Goldenfield, *Cogito* editors and university instructors in, respectively, gender studies and German transcendental idealism, do not express amusement. In fact, MacLane's gender-ambiguous face expresses contempt.

"Like what?" she snaps.

In the moment, Digby is more struck by the click of her hard consonants that suggest she grew up in South Jersey than by the need to field her question appropriately, whatever that may be.

"Oh, personal abduction," Digby says mildly, then adds, "or maybe just some routine plunder," in hope that this addition has a mollifying effect.

Fortunately, his hostess finds his retort droll, or so she says, and this seems to put an end—for now, at least—to any more quizzing from the gender philosopher. This gives Digby the opportunity to excuse himself and head for the Victorian lavatory, fingering the roach in his jacket pocket all the way. He tokes up as soon as the door is closed and locked.

About Digby's panic: this welcoming party merely touches the tip of the angst iceberg that chills his soul. The bigger picture is that he is a forty-three-year-old man who has been unemployed for more than a year, and is now flying solo and by the seat of his pants in a small Vermont college town with a commission for which he is totally unqualified—at least as far as he can determine. Because the truth of the matter is he has only a feeble glimmering of what it is he is supposed to do here.

I am an impostor. A charlatan. A quack in tweeds.

But this should not be any cause for panic because it is not as though Digby is living in fear of being found out. He was already found out before he ever pulled off Route 9 into Louden one day ago. Everyone at the party knows his quack status, except, possibly, the hostess who also happens to be the heiress of Bonner Hastings III, the late founder and bank-roller of *Cogito*. Digby is here at Felicia's pleasure.

So his panic must have deeper origins and Digby suspects they may be existential. In the three weeks prior to his job interview, Digby subjected himself to a crash course in the history of philosophy, hair-raising in both its speed and super-ficiality. He did not linger over concepts he could not grasp, which were well more than half of them. His only lingering was over certain passages in a refresher titled, *The Essential Søren Kierkegaard*. These passages spoke—in translation from the Danish—to his panic. Apparently, panic-struck angst is not that rare and is never very pretty. Digby found this somewhat reassuring but also sickening, a word the frail Dane threw around liberally, especially in his dense, headache-inducing tract, *The Sickness Unto Death*, an analysis of the inherent tension between the 'finite self' and the 'infinite self,' neither of which Digby could locate in his own self with any clarity.

Digby was also struck by the fact that Kierkegaard adopted the pseudonym, 'Anti-Climacus,' as his byline for *Sickness*. It was definitely a catchy alias, suggesting a dogged self who just can't bring himself—or for that matter, Mrs. Kierkegaard, if there was one—to a satisfying conclusion. Did Søren mean it as a gag? Was this Danish humor? Several years earlier, when Digby was still employed writing his "Proximo" column for *New York Magazine*, he pronounced the clubs of Copenhagen to be on the cutting edge of the contemporary jazz scene; in the piece, he quoted one Danish jazz club owner as saying,

"Some people have a problem putting the idea that we are known as Jolly Danes together with the fact that we have the highest suicide rate in Europe. It's easy—all Danes who aren't jolly commit suicide." It was a Danish joke.

According to Kierkegaard-qua-Anti-Climacus, panic is basic to the human condition even if one is fraud-free; all it takes to go to pieces is to tune in to one's mortality. Yet, says Søren, our mortality is exactly what we should be focusing on because therein lies enlightenment. It was at this point that Digby tuned out and turned to something more uplifting, *The Essential Immanuel Kant*. Based on past experience, Digby has found that thinking about his inevitable demise makes him feel paralyzed, totally lifeless, and hopeless. *Yes, Anti-Climacus, consciousness of one's mortality is the mother of all panics, so who needs it?*

Mortality aside, Digby's finite self, the one that in its fifth decade is trying to restart his career, remains beside itself with panic, especially because it is attempting to restart his life as a quack. Thus Digby's need to inhabit a chemically spawned alternate universe, if only for an hour or two at a dinner party, is self-evident.

Speaking of which, there is nothing quite as self-evident as the fragrance of burning marijuana in an enclosure the size of a Victorian lavatory. There was a time when lighting up a Camel or better yet, a Gauloise, was sufficient to mask the smell of pot in a bathroom, but those days have been rendered obsolete by the coequal disgrace of generating tobacco smoke just about anywhere. In any event, Digby left his pack of Parliament Lights in his car.

For a split second, Digby experiences a memory glimpse of the golden boy he once was, a modern-day Nostradamus of pop-cult with jobs on trendy magazines his for the asking, well-dressed women undressing in front of him in finely appointed hotel rooms as merely one of his rewards. "But it's not too late!" he says to himself more loudly than a man talking to himself in a first floor bathroom of a guest-filled house should.

Steam! A high wattage inspiration sizzles his mind. Although he was a middling student in the two introductory philosophy courses he took in college, he did have a gift for physics and he now recalls that droplets of heated water are an excellent odor sponge. Happily, the Hastings made an exception to their period design and installed one of those one-piece vinyl showers in the corner of their Victorian lav. He opens its glass door and spins the hot faucet to full throttle. Within minutes, the tiny room is flush with fog, a virtual Russian sweat bath. He inhales deeply. There is still a touch of the old ganja in the atmosphere so he opens the oak medicine chest and seizes a bottle of eau de cologne. He *shpritzes.* Genius! Every breath is breathtakingly perfumed. Without doubt, he has just invented a room deodorizer of stupendous proportions. If he could only figure out how to market it, he could walk away from this absurd job before it begins.

There is a knock on the lavatory door. A voice: "Everything okay in there, Mr. Maxwell?"

It is the voice of Madeleine Follet, the magazine's long-standing office manager.

"Tip top," Digby answers through the door. "Why do you ask?"

"Steam," comes Madeleine's reply. "It's kinda puffing through the bottom of the door. And sneezing. Lots of sneezing out here."

"I see," he says. "No problem. Be right out."

Digby is abruptly and gratefully cold sober. In rapid sequence, he turns off the shower, replaces the bottle of eau in the cabinet, then finds and switches on the ventilation fan. He is ready to make new friends.

But first, a quick touch-up of his persona. He rubs the fog off the sink mirror with his tweed sleeve. There is apparently more touching-up to be done than he anticipated. His face is beaded with odor-absorbing droplets, his hair hangs like a soggy Victorian fringe over his eyebrows, his newly bought Brooks Brothers button-down, although advertised as wash-and-dry, has acquired the texture of a crepe tunic, and his tweed sleeves, especially the one from which his right hand emerges—the hand with which he manipulated the shower faucet—has the weftage of a spring terrier paddling in a mill-stream.

He pats his face dry with toilet paper. Then, seeing that bits of the paper stick to his mug like mini-distress flags, he rubs his face with a linen guest towel. He decides to leave the rest as is. Actually, the fringed-forehead effect strikes him as dramatically appealing, like the coiffeur of a knight's page in a medieval miracle play.

Digby's hostess and her guests are silently waiting for him in the dining room. With the exception of Ms. MacLane who gives him a fisheye, they courteously ignore his entrance and sit mutely as he takes the only vacant chair, the one catty-corner to Felicia Hastings.

"I kind of got carried away in there," he says cheerfully to all assembled. "It's so fresh up here in the mountains. So clean. And I detected some Manhattan grime still clinging to me."

And that does the trick. Immediately chatter resumes, a few smiles are posted in his direction, and Mrs. Hastings calls over her shoulder for the soup course to be brought to table by the help—a wan blonde wearing a smart pants suit. In truth, the ease with which he has just covered his ass does not surprise Digby: since he was a young boy he has had a talent for the heartfelt yet totally nebulous excuse. He has always known intuitively that form trumps content in interpersonal relations.

Indeed, with the ice broken and his brain back in gear, he is able to make small talk and listen attentively to his tablemates, MacLane, Goldenfield, Madeleine Follet, and this Russian fellow sitting across from him, a visiting scholar who occasionally speaks in an indecipherable blend of syntactical enigmatology and logical notation. Digby even gets off a wee bit of wit here and there as they go from butternut squash soup to chicken croquettes to watercress salad. This isn't so hard, he thinks, *I am, after all, a professional bullshitter.*

After coffee and apple crumble a la mode are served, Felicia taps her spoon against her cup. The chitchat stops and she speaks.

"When Bonner knew that he did not have much time left with us, he asked me to bring a chair next to his bed and—well—to take dictation." Here the widow pauses to smile from face to face. "He was bossy to the end, my Bonner!"

All titter appreciatively.

"Bonner's last wish was the same as his lifelong wish—to ensure that his magazine would carry on. *Cogito* was, in a sense, his child." Again, she pauses and looks down, it seems, in the direction of her womb, the organ that did not produce any siblings to rival *Cogito*. "But old fashioned as he was—and I am told Bonner was old fashioned since he was a toddler—he always had respect for new forms of thinking, new sensibilities, and most importantly, new ways of doing philosophy. He was a classicist and an Aristotelian to the end, but he always insisted that if Aristotle were alive today, he would have his own blog, 'Some Particulars About Universals dot com.'"

Digby leads the laughter this time, in part because he always enjoys hearing himself quoted.

"Bonner told me that even if he had been well, he would have been unable on his own to push *Cogito* in the direction he wanted it to go," Felicia continues, producing a leather-bound notebook from her lap, opening it, and beginning to read. "'My mission has always been to make philosophy accessible to the general reader. But I have lost touch with who that general reader is. What animates him. What questions bedevil him.'

"And that is why Bonner wanted me to find a successor whose roots were in the culture at large. An editor of *Cogito* who comes to philosophy from the outside in. A man who starts with the questions that thinking people in the twenty-first century are asking and then seeks the philosophers and philosophies that respond to them. In short, a man exactly like Digby Maxwell."

Although Felicia Hastings' speech and the graceful nod in his direction that follows it were obviously rehearsed, Digby finds himself full of admiration for the old girl. Not just by her articulateness, but by the power of her loyalty to her late husband. Marital loyalty, in Digby's personal experience, is quaintly old fashioned.

Clearly, it is his turn to speak. He swallows hard. He smiles.

"I am an impostor," he begins. Digby finds that he is at his best in this sort of situation if he starts right off by tying himself in a knot; he believes it stimulates his right brain. "In fact, I undoubtedly know less about formal philosophy than anyone in this room. But being an impostor is a condition that all of us suffer from to some degree or another in a Kierkegaardian sense. We live in an age of massive denial. And so perhaps the impostor's trick of improvising can prove particularly valuable at this time and in this venture."

Digby has only the vaguest idea of what he is talking about, but one thing about his right brain is that it is fluent, undisturbed by logic. Sensing that his audience—well, most of it—is grooving to his performance, he runs on for a while, managing to cram both Mickey Mouse and Ralph Waldo Emerson into one daredevil sentence, and YouTube, steroids, and Foucault into another. By the conclusion of his pell-mell peroration he appears to have won over some of the skeptics in the crowd including, to his astonishment, himself. He feels competent, up to snuff, in charge.

"Let's start off with a brainstorming session in my office tomorrow morning at ten," he says, then adds, "We will *cogito* outside of the box."

CHAPTER 2

Back in the eighth and ninth decades of the final century of the last millennium—the 1980's and '90's—Digby was indeed a writer and editor to be reckoned with in that epicenter of media cool, Manhattan, New York. His beat was "the very next thing" and, first at *The Village Voice* and then at *New York Magazine*, he informed hungry-to-be-in-the-know readers what, undetected by their radar, was coming down the pike. He perceived hip social trends that, at the moment of his writing, were no more than whispered phrases in NoHo coffee shops or casual gestures in Bed-Stuy schoolyards. He identified regional garage bands that would go gold in six months' time; he predicted what obscure party drug would be *de rigeur* by the upcoming New Year's Eve. It was a gift he had and he was extravagantly paid for it.

The source of this talent, he believes, is his aptitude for empathy, albeit empathy in the service of exploiting rather than helping his fellow man. He picked up quickening vibes where others only picked up cacophony; he detected subconscious whims in the unconscious masses.

By way of illustration, consider the daytime quiz show, *Family Feud*. On the surface, the show seems just another vehicle for numbing the mind, eating up thirty minutes of pained, day-to-day consciousness. But *Family Feud* has astounding levels, levels that undoubtedly escape the notice of cognitive psychologists who should know better.

On the show, two teams of contestants—loosely related family members—attempt to guess the most popular responses to survey questions that previously have been posed to average Americans. Questions like, "Name something that you are most likely to find in a diaper bag." But here is the tricky part: to guess correctly, it doesn't help at all to know what the most common items found in American diaper bags actually are. No, what one needs to know is what the average American *thinks* are the most common items found in American diaper bags. Major distinction. The winners are not people with encyclopedic knowledge of American habits; they are people who can guess what the average American thinks average American habits are. Astounding levels indeed. For here is where *Family Feud* becomes deliciously tricky: the absolutely best contestants are people who simply live and think like average Americans, people who automatically figure that the items found in *their* diaper bags are what the pollees imagine are in the average American's diaper bag. These contestants cut through the levels and eliminate the guesswork; they are wise to their averageness.

Digby is a whiz at playing *Family Feud* in front of his TV, stoned or straight. He flips his neural switch and he becomes an average American, peeks into his or her diaper bag as easily as he can peek into his own underwear. But unlike the winning families on *Family Feud*, Digby is also blessed with the ability to take this to the next step: he can intuit the average American's habits and tastes before the average American is fully aware of them himself. He is a beat ahead of the average man's self-consciousness. It is a kind of time-travel empathy.

Feedback loop that the media is, Digby's job only got easier as his reputation spread. If he slipped the term "mall chick" into his weekly column, the expression became common parlance at New York dinner tables the following week. By predicting that it would become the term *du jour*, Digby made it into the term *du jour*. He *was* the very next thing.

All of this, of course, gradually went to his head. Not a whit did it matter to him that his particular talent was on the same level as some village drunk who has a knack for picking winners at the dog races. On the contrary, Digby started to feel positively papal in his infallibility. He began to strut his stuff. He held forth at cocktail parties, projecting an aura of in-the-knowness. Along the way, he regularly bedded pretty young things who saw in him a crystal ball of lifestyle secrets that could ratchet up the style of their lacking lives. It was a *quid pro quo* arrangement: in exchange for a tip on the very next fashion trend they took off their clothes.

Digby was well aware that he partook of this indulgence in spite of his personal moral guidelines. These had been shaped by the minor, practical-minded philosopher, Nelson Algren, who once astutely wrote, "Never, never—no matter what else you do in your whole life—*never* sleep with anyone whose troubles are worse than your own." (This philosophical predilection of Digby's, he subsequently learned, plants him squarely in the tradition of Jamesian American Pragmatism.) In truth, these young women invariably had troubles worse than his own, including the troubles that come automatically from bedding down with a married man.

Incrementally, Digby was becoming insufferable—right up to the point when he became a total shithead.

At the time, this didn't bother him in the least. Among the consolations of being a shithead is one's liberation from common moral standards, not to mention other people's regard. It did, however, bother Fanny, so she did what any modern woman with an ounce of self-respect would have done: she divorced Digby. It was not the infidelities that tipped the balance, she informed him, it was that he had outlived his usefulness as a member of the family. (This places her in the Benthamite Utilitarian school.) Of course, Fanny knew that this assessment would hurt him, that is, as much as anything possibly could hurt him at that time; if nothing else, Digby still aspired to being useful.

To be fair to all concerned, Fanny and Digby's marriage never suffered the common fate of passion run out of steam, because there was never much steam there to begin with. They married soon after Digby snagged his first job as a columnist and Fanny graduated from law school, a period in their young lives when they both were full of promise and promise was what mattered most.

Indeed, they were typical of their generation, taking what they considered a mature, long-range view of their union. It was akin to buying hog belly futures. Fanny, who was a gifted list and chart maker, filled legal pads with two-, five-, and ten-year plans for their joint journey, while Digby, who depended on the general unpredictability of the future for his livelihood, looked over her shoulder with admiration and alarm. Despite his aptitude for forecasting popular tastes, Digby had always viewed his own future as a region cluttered with trapdoors. He looked to his bride for leadership.

Their sex life was only a tad better than adequate, but that mattered far less than the fact that together they would become a Manhattan couple to be reckoned with, a duo on the move. It was an arranged marriage which they had arranged themselves. And so for Fanny to ultimately break up the partnership on the basis of failed utility made perfect sense. Then again, if she had not happened to spot Digby exiting the Gramercy Park Hotel one late October afternoon, his left hand cupping the right cheek of a twenty-something's buttocks, she may have made do with a lower standard of utility.

For reasons that only a true shithead can fully appreciate, Fanny's rejection pained Digby less than when, only a few months afterward, the managing editor of New York Magazine, Scott Kravitz, informed him that his gift for spotting the very next thing had not aged well and furthermore that his prose had become far too snarky for both him and their readers. Even worse, said Scott, was that the writers to whom Digby assigned articles were deeply unhappy with his management style; "insufferable" was a word that popped up frequently in their complaints. Digby's days as New York's preeminent trend maven were numbered and those numbers were already down to two digits, Scott informed him.

"Jesus, Scott, I didn't see this coming," Digby sputtered.

"My point exactly," Scott retorted.

"Maybe I've been a bit distracted lately," Digby pleaded. "You know, the divorce and all." Unlike many men, Digby has no problem humbling himself before other males. Even groveling is not beneath him. To him, groveling just feels like getting down on the floor and goofing around like a puppy, although that may be why his style of groveling rarely achieves its desired effect.

"I don't think it's that," Scott said. "It's an age thing. I've always seen you as a sort of romantic poet of the zeitgeist and, as we all know, romantic poets burn out young."

"That's because they die young."

"Well, then, do take care of yourself, Digby."

Yes, groveling Digby does shamelessly, but he draws the line at being on the receiving end of ironic pity.

"Actually, I do have a final report from the zeitgeist for you, Scott," he said. "In less than a year your whole fucking magazine is going to be dead meat. Your baby boomer readers have more hair growing out of their ears than they have on their heads. Your best option would be to merge with *Modern Maturity*."

Digby actually did have his finger on something here, although he did not know the half of it until several months later. His dismissal from New York Magazine *coincided with a sharp downturn in the popularity of print periodicals all over the map as blogs and Twitter literally altered the dimension of time. Gossip became an echo chamber in one's hip pocket Blackberry; the moment a trend gained traction, it was instantly sooo last year, sooo last week, sooo last nanosecond. The very next thing was happening now or, at times, had already happened.*

Of course, Digby had seen the digital communications revolution coming down the pike for years. What he had failed to envision was its potential for wiping him out.

Digby started working his Rolodex (another item on the brink of extinction) the morning after Scott dumped him. Right off, he phoned Phil Winston, owner and editor-in-chief of *The Village Voice*, reaching him at his high command hot tub in his SoHo penthouse. Not surprisingly, Phil already knew why he was calling. "Bummer," was his greeting.

"I guess it's time for me to come home to the *Voice*," Digby said cheerily.

"I hear you," Phil said.

"So, what do you say?"

"We've got this kid, you know. Billy Fairchild. Answers to 'Nappy.' Nappy Napp. It's a hip-hop thingy."

"I've always been in favor of diversity."

"Napp has his hand on the pulse of America," Phil went on. "He feels the vibes. He talks the talk. You know?"

Digby knew.

In the moment, he also remembered that Phil was the main reason he had left the *Voice* in the first place. The heir to a mineral mining fortune, Phil suffered from trust fund guilt and was trying to overcome it by becoming hipper than hip, which in his case meant buying a downtown newspaper with his unearned cash and assigning articles that blasted corporate life. Phil wore his unwashed sandy hair down to his shoulders and usually sported a denim shirt open to his sternum and paint-spattered jeans. (There was a great deal of speculation in the *Voice*'s offices about who, exactly, had furnished the splatter; the good money was on 'Mr. Z.,' a popular graffiti artist of the day who was known to do just about anything for a buck.) And, of course, Phil spoke hipster-stoner talk, or at least his quaint version of it that made him sound like a recent immigrant who had taken an ESL course from a superannuated hippie.

After reading *Existentialism in a Nutshell* during his auto-tutorial marathon, Digby discovered that he is definitely not of the Jean-Paul Sartre school of persona-hood. J-P believed that role-playing, be it as a Paris waiter or a New York hipster, is *"pour soi,"* that it is treating oneself as an object rather than as a subject. *Très unauthentique.* True enough, Jean-Paul, but to Digby's mind role-playing sure as hell is the most efficient way to get through a day, especially if that day involves any face-to-face contact. This marks Digby as more of an American Pragmatist than a French Existentialist and therefore he has an unusually high tolerance for phonies. But there are limits to Digby's tolerance and his was reached when an old friend informed him that Phil secretly dined at the Yale Club every Friday night where he hobnobbed with bankers and mutual fund analysts. Therefore Digby is probably closer to Sartre than he originally thought: they both draw the line somewhere.

"Is Nappy a Yalie?" Digby asked Phil.

He heard some hot tub splish and splash before Phil grunted "Good luck" and hung up.

Digby worked his way down his call list, ending with *New Jersey Magazine*, a monthly that regularly features top ten lists—The Top Ten New Jersey Dentists, Casinos, Bar Mitzvah Venues, etc. In Digby's phone interview, NJM's editor-in-chief gently suggested that Digby was a tad over the hill for their super cool enterprise.

Washed up was he.

It was at this time that Digby rekindled his college hobby of smoking pot, usually starting with his morning coffee. This practice was, of course, an escape. It helped him keep the reality of his new situation in the same remote area of his brain as the names of his kindergarten classmates and the members of the Supreme Court. Yet with his inherently slippery self coupled with his inherited bent for metaphysics (a propensity he was not yet aware of), stoned reality struck him as having no less validity than everyday, non-stoned reality. For a man who routinely saw the world from other people's points of view, the view through a haze of marijuana seemed just another reality.

This was later confirmed by Digby's sniff through the works of Thomas De Quincey, a nineteenth-century British philosopher and opium aficionado. De Quincey made the stunning observation that what actually made him high on his favorite drug was the *contrast* of altered consciousness with his normal consciousness. So if one were high on opium all the time, that would become his normal consciousness and no kick would he get. A case in point is the first importation of Indian tea—*Camellia sinensis*—to England. British intelligentsia wrote rhapsodic chapbooks detailing hallucinations and transcendental insights occasioned by just one cup of the stuff. Yet by the end of the 1800's, when every Brit was downing several cups of tea daily, tea consciousness had become normal consciousness, and that consciousness was nothing to write home about.

Actually, it was worse than that. What Digby had forgotten (and perhaps De Quincey never knew) is that once drug-induced reality becomes *basic* reality, feelings of transcendent happiness take a precipitous nosedive. Being high leads to being low. It is the psychic equivalent of physics' Law of Conservation of Energy (i.e., the amount of energy in the universe is fixed and cannot be created or destroyed). Ditto for bliss. If one uses up his fixed allotment on an excellent drug trip, sooner or later he pays for it double in melancholy. Thus did Digby's renewed hobby increasingly and ineluctably lead him into the dark room of despair and panic.

The exact location of this room was on the second floor of 145 Bleecker Street where Digby's boyhood friend and pot connection, Asim Moustavavi, rented him his sofa after Digby could no longer afford to pay the tab at the residence hotel to which he had decamped after Fanny sent him packing. Asim gave him a package deal for both the sofa and a weekly supply of Buenos Aires Red.

Digby was a quiet guest. He often spent several days in a row without leaving the apartment. His days developed a certain rhythm: late morning coffee and a few tokes, TV talk shows and a few more tokes, a nap, preparing dinner for Asim and himself accompanied by several additional tokes.

Occasionally, he would vary his routine by playing a trippy game of his own invention that he called, "Me Too." Clad in T-shirt and boxers, a cup of Asim's superb espresso in hand, he would stare out the front window onto the street below where West Village folk of a grand variety of ages, races, and genders would be parading by. Digby would select one of these pedestrians and fix his gaze upon him or her. And then he would perform his little trick: he would *become* that person. Slip into that person's self.

Mind you, this would be a *full* slip, empathy on a Husserlian scale. As Fanny was wont to remind Digby, his talent for personal identification with complete strangers is born of his nebulous selfhood. With no 'there' there, assuming another's identity is a piece of cake—there is no self to transcend before making the leap. Digby would not only inhabit the body of the selected stranger in the street, he would experience his emotions, his loves and hates, his responses to his environment, his entire worldview.

Do I have time for a mocha latte? Digby would ask as he inhabited the frantic, sharp-featured young man in a lime green polo shirt striding down Bleecker. *Maybe just a half-and-half. I don't want to be wired for my meeting with Clarence.*

It was a soothing exercise for Digby, at once transcendent and mundane. At the very least, here and there it kept his mind off his own prospects for a few minutes.

Another activity Digby added to his day was watching for the arrival of the mailman, then meeting him in the foyer and relieving him of Asim's mail, which he then took upstairs and read in the kitchen. And so it was one afternoon, leafing through Asim's newly arrived copy of the Louden College alumni magazine that, on the same page as personal ads of

Louden grads seeking companionship that may or may not lead to a romantic relationship, Digby spotted a headline at the top of an advertisement situated inside a death notice-like plain black border:

Independent Philosophy Magazine Seeks Editor-in-Chief
Background in Contemporary Culture
Primary Requirement

Digby giggled, a rare occurrence in those days. *What exactly would a* dependent *philosophy magazine consist of? Would it contain infomercials written by wealthy Kantian lobbyists?*

Obviously, the 'primary requirement' bit caught Digby's eye too; but at the time it only reanimated his old amused condescension toward out-of-touch academic types, that is, reanimated it right up until that recess of his brain that was still informed about his current lifestyle spoke up, saying, in effect, *Who the fuck are you to condescend to anybody, loser?*

Digby abruptly tucked Asim's alum mag under more pressing mail, which included an overdue electric bill, and opted once again for chemical aid in quieting that know-it-all scold inside his head.

Sometime later, during his three-week, ADD-ish philosophy study marathon, Digby was struck by how often the concept of fate popped up, whacking against the concept of redemption once he began reading the big Christian thinkers. Apparently if everything is predestined, it is hard to make a case for mending one's ways and making a fresh start. No matter what you do, *que sera, sera.* It is all an appointment in Samarra. Nonetheless, for several days after reading that advertisement, Digby was visited by the thought that not only had Fate put that magazine in his hands, but he may have just been offered a once-in-a-lifetime chance to redeem himself. Digby was not usually given to such magical thinking; he always considered such thinking as the last refuge of a desperate man. But, of course, Digby was a desperate man.

So late one morning he wrapped his supply of Buenos Aires Red in tinfoil and hid it from himself in an urn in Asim's bedroom. He typed up a charming letter of personal introduction to the address listed at the bottom of the black box, then folded in a half-dozen Xeroxed copies of his best columns, including his most celebrated *New York Magazine* piece about the zeitgeist connection between Dungeons and Dragons and Hershey Kiss Lip Gloss. A few days later he received a two-line note from a Mrs. Felicia Hastings of Louden, Vermont, requesting his presence at the Harvard Club of New York for an interview in two weeks.

Mrs. H. met Digby in the club's foyer, led him to the club's dining room and, although Digby would have preferred a double scotch straight up, ordered coffees for both of them. She looked him over silently for several minutes. He was wearing the tan linen suit Fanny had selected for him for a National Magazine Awards dinner several years back and he looked, he thought, award-winning. Mrs. Hastings, on the other hand, was wearing a severe, navy blue skirt suit edged in inky black piping, giving her the aspect of a chiaroscuro etching. She withdrew a copy of *Cogito* from her handbag and handed it across the table to Digby.

It had the same heft and trim size as *Reader's Digest*s of yore, also the same bible-like typeface on the cover listing the articles inside. The lead piece was titled, "The Ethics of Ambiguity"; next came, "The Metaphysical Conception of Analyticity"; then the most mind-numbing of the lot, "Zombies and Consciousness."

Despite his recent study marathon, Digby could no more guess what these articles might be about than he could supply the Latin name for the fern hanging from the wall behind Mrs. Hastings' head. His first instinct was to excuse himself for a trip to the men's room, toward which he would casually saunter before tear-assing out the club's front door. He held that option in check for the moment.

"What's your first impression?" Mrs. Hastings asked in a rather studied nonchalant tone.

"Boring," Digby replied, not only matching her tone, but trumping it with a raised eyebrow. He would have liked to have been able to say that this impression of hauteur was part of his interview strategy, but it was the portraits of those grim, former Harvard presidents on the club's darksome, oak-paneled walls that inspired it. Digby is extremely impressionable.

"What would you rather see on the cover?"

"A picture," Digby said. "Possibly of a beautiful woman, say, reading Sartre in a Paris café."

"In a short skirt, no doubt."

"Mr. Sartre?"

"You disappoint me, Mr. Maxwell," Mrs. Hastings responded. "We are looking for a relevant philosophy magazine, not a tawdry one."

"I guess the question is, relevant to whom?" Digby said. This is what is known in the trade as treading water.

"I read your piece about Dungeons and Dragons," Mrs. Hastings went on. "I don't have the vaguest idea of what it was about."

"Dungeons is a game millions of people play. A role-playing game. At the heart of it is the unpredictability of events. The game probably says more about randomness than Aristotle could have imagined."

This, of course, was Digby's famous right brain blabbing, albeit a right brain recently schooled by *Philosophy for Dummies*. Clearly the time was nigh for him to execute his men's room trick.

But hold the phone! Was that a twinkle Digby detected in the old girl's eyes?

"Bonner—Mr. Hastings—once said that if Aristotle were alive today he would be hooked up on the Internet," she said, exposing a row of surprisingly young-looking teeth with a half-smile.

"He would probably have his own blog. 'Some Particulars About Universals dot com,'" Digby said in a blink. His right brain is a wondrous thing.

Mrs. Hastings' smile expanded. "We are offering seventy-five thousand a year with a comfortable apartment included," she said.

Was that it? Was she actually offering Digby the job before their coffees had even arrived?

It should be noted that had Digby been even a fraction less desperate, he would have smelled something fish-like in Mrs. Hastings' instantaneous offer. But desperate is as Digby does.

"Yup," was all he could manage to reply.

"Can you begin in two weeks?"

He could.

And that is when his panic commenced in earnest.

Digby dug around in Asim's urn the moment he got back to his apartment.

Chapter 3

"Okay, picture this fellow Joe sitting in front of his TV late on a Tuesday evening. His wife has already gone to bed. The Knicks game is over and he switches off the set. He feels uneasy, too uneasy to go up to bed just yet, even though he has to start getting ready for work in only six hours. He asks himself what the hell it is that he's uneasy about. He's got a reasonably good job. He has a house, a wife, a kid, a dog. But something's not right with Joe. Then he hears himself mumbling, 'The point of it all is . . . The point of it all is . . .'"

Digby stops talking here and tries to make eye contact with his staff. Only one is willing to reciprocate, Madeleine, who appears to be stirred by his opening sally, although it may be his seeming cluelessness that stirs her. The other three, June MacLane, Elliot Goldenfield, and the Russian logician whose name, Digby believes, begins with an 'R,' make eye contact with the floor.

The floor *is* impressive. It is made of dark, broad board hemlock and is covered, for the most part, by a faded, crimson-and-amber Soumak rug. The seats upon which the staff has parked themselves for this, their first meeting with Digby, are a pair of plushy, tufted Victorian settees. Digby sits behind a long oak desk in a swivel chair, also oak, that is fitted with a leather pillow. The velvet-draped, floor-to-ceiling window on his right looks out onto a great sward of budding wildflowers and then onto a grand lawn that, in the far distance, merges with the central quad of Louden College. Collectively, the five of them look like a washed-out turn-of-the-century painting of themselves.

"So," Digby continues. "What can we tell Joe that will give him a handle on things?"

"Things?" Goldenfield chimes back. "What sort of *things?*"

"Exactly," Digby says. "What sort of things?"

"I'm afraid you've lost me," Goldenfield simpers.

Elliot Goldenfield is a lanky fellow, covered from cuff to collar in brown corduroy, his thick black hair slicked straight back in a style befitting this nineteenth-century executive suite.

Digby's guess is that Goldenfield enjoys a private fantasy about his ancestry, one that reaches back to the court of St. James. He reminds Digby of a young man named Jack Collier who lived across the hall in his Swarthmore dormitory. Collier was also tall, angular, and imposing. President of the Equestrian Club and treasurer of the Fencing Club, Jack was given to wearing paisley bow ties and a black cashmere topcoat. He cut a fine figure, so to speak, and the other Swarthmore students, mostly nerds and smartasses, regarded him with awe and sniggers.

Then one day when Collier's roommate, Mickey Bernstein, was picking up the mail, he noticed a letter addressed to their room to one Jack Cohen. It was from the B'nai B'rith Youth Organization in Cleveland, Jack Collier's hometown. It took Mickey about fifteen minutes on the Net to verify that Collier and Cohen were one and the same. But Swarthmore students being clever little bastards, none of them confronted Jack with this discovery; no, their tack was to tag along behind him on the way to the dining hall quipping, "Man, look at that pine tree. What beautiful *pine colliers!*" and "Anybody up for an *ice cream collier* after dinner?" Terribly cruel, but funny too, in a collegiate assholey sort of way. Digby was alone among his friends in feeling that Jack was perfectly entitled to assume any identity that got him through the day. Even then Digby believed that all identities were arbitrary at best, so why the fuss? It was one of the few choices a person had.

"Well, Elliot, I bet this Joe person is anxious," Madeleine offers, then adds, "You know, *angst*."

Madeleine is a Louden local with only a Louden High School education, but she had been Bonner Hastings' amanuensis since the first issue of *Cogito* some thirty years ago and therefore has picked up a veritable unabridged dictionary of philo-lingo. Hers is by far the most eager and open face in the room and Digby smiles at her, hoping that she, at least, will be his ally here.

"He has psychology problem," says the Russian, still not looking up from the rug. "But philosophical not."

"Kierkegaard wrote about anxiety," Madeleine says brightly.

"So he is psychologist!" snaps the Russian.

"Maybe your Joe has an identity problem," says Ms. Mac-Lane. These are the first even remotely sociable words out of her mouth since Digby met her at Mrs. Hastings' home the previous evening. It takes him only a moment to figure out what has brought her into the conversation—the possibility that Joe has a gender identity problem.

"That's true," Digby says tentatively. "Joe doesn't know who he is. Or possibly *what* he is."

"That would not make him particularly unusual in the postmodern world," replies Ms. MacLane.

Instead of listening closely to her words, Digby finds himself studying the area above MacLane's upper lip. He detects a few wiry hairs that he suspects have been tenderly cultivated there. They lend a certain Groucho Marxist aspect to her countenance. Back in Manhattan, Digby had acquaintances and friends on every point of the LGBT spectrum and, especially as a man with what his ex-wife termed, 'a transpersonal condition,' he did not find their orientations in the least disorienting. But MacLane's childlike and petulant earnestness regarding her L-ness strikes him as provincial. Perhaps that is because she is stranded here in the provinces.

"So, who or what do you suppose this Joe person is?" Digby finally says.

"It obviously depends on who defines him," says MacLane.

"For starters, let's say Joe, himself," Digby replies.

"Well, since you obviously have a more intimate relationship with this fellow than anyone else here, I suggest *you* tell us how Joe defines himself," Goldenfield says dryly.

Without a moment's thought, Digby says, "Joe defines himself as a guy who just had his first glimpse of his mortality."

Digby regrets his blurt immediately. To begin with, his identification with this Joe Everyman is way too blatant, not to mention needy, and at this point can only further undermine his already tenuous hold on leadership. But more worrisome is the fact that, inadvertently, he is spouting words that are perilously close to philosophy talk. That is not what Felicia Hastings brought him a hundred and fifty miles due north to spout. She brought him here to burrow from the outside in.

"We already did an issue that focused on mortality," Madeleine says helpfully. "June, 1991. Heidegger, Camus. And some Aristotle too, of course. Bonner's favorite."

Thank God for that, Digby thinks. He has had enough thoughts about his mortality to last him a lifetime. Now where the hell was he going with this? Last night, stretched out on an absolutely divine divan in his three-room apartment one flight up from *Cogito's* offices in what is known as Hastings Towers, he had channeled his Joe straight out of *Family Feud*; and inside Joe's existential diaper bag was some nasty dread, the kind that stinks up everybody's existential diaper bag whether or not they have an advanced degree in philosophy. At the time, the Joe 'what's-the-point-of-it-all?' scenario had struck Digby as brilliant, a delicate balance between the concerns of the man in the street and the man in the Acropolis. But now Digby has a sinking feeling that is, he believes, unrelated to his recurring tingles of mortality; it has more to do with hanging on to his new divan while he is still on this side of the Great Divide. He reaches back to his *New York Magazine* headset. He improvises.

"Joe wants to go to heaven," he blurts out. "He's wondering what it's like and what his odds are of getting in."

The Russian snorts. Goldenfield rolls his eyes, well, heavenward.

"Eighty-two percent of Americans believe in heaven," Digby continues. As of yore, tossing off made-up statistics gives him strength; it lubricates his way to pure bullshit. "They want to know what's cooking up there. Who's invited. What they're serving. Living accommodations."

"I hope you are not serious, Mr. Maxwell," June MacLane says.

"Please call me Digby," Digby replies pleasantly. "And yes, I am serious. Our next issue will be devoted in its entirety to the idea of heaven."

Without a moment's reflection, Digby has made this decision and made it public. In truth, he didn't even see it coming. It was inspired.

"Fairy story," the Russian says.

Greatness! Just the reaction Digby was hoping for. He feels he is on the right track at last. He suddenly remembers the Russian's name.

"That is true, Rostislav," Digby says. "But then again, so is the subject of good and evil, is it not so?"

When talking to foreigners, Digby often finds himself unconsciously mimicking their jumbled syntax. In any event, and certainly without realizing it, Digby has shut the Russian up by citing a fundamental dictum of logical positivism, namely that the whole enterprise of moral philosophy is about as rationally based as "Snow White and the Seven Dwarfs"—or heaven, for that matter. Out of the corner of his eye, Digby observes that Madeleine offers Rostislav a consoling smile, not that he believes the Russian needs or has ever needed one.

"There is a line," Goldenfield begins, looking at Digby with a mix of incredulity and pity. "A line that separates subjects worthy of serious thought and subjects that are, in a word, trivial. I do not believe that Bonner Hastings ever intended us to cross that line."

"It's hard to know what Bonner thinks at this point. Anyone know a good medium?" Digby says jauntily. He is convinced that he has found the perfect voice for his new vocation, never mind that it is also a voice that may convince his employees that he is several categories short of an imperative. He quickly goes on. "Sometimes treating a trivial subject thoughtfully produces fascinating results. In any event, eighty-two percent of would-be heaven dwellers do not consider it trivial in the least."

Digby is getting his first whiff of insurrection. It has a foul, gassy smell. Nobody says a word.

"Let's give it a try," Digby says, trying to inflect a few pleading tones into his voice. "Float the idea with our smartest contributors. Get some feedback. And try to think of some non-academics who might have something interesting to say on the subject—poets, priests—." He stops himself before adding, 'rock stars,' but he does say, "Does anybody here read *Rolling Stone?*"

Surprisingly, Madeleine raises her hand. Hope springs.

"Let's reconvene in a couple of days," Digby says and his staff rises and vacates in a platonic minute.

Digby spends the next three hours pouring over two boxes of past editions of *Cogito*, a reassuringly soporific experience. He tries to imagine who exactly reads this stuff beside the loved ones of the articles' authors. Other philosophy types, to be sure, but just how many of them can there be? At Swarthmore, there were no more than half a dozen tenured philosophy professors on staff, and two of those, he recalls, only read philosophers who wrote in Greek or Latin. Of course, niche publications are the new wave, running on the steam of niche products; and indeed, the back cover and last three pages of *Cogito* contain ads for new books from university presses with titles like *Inference from Signs*, *Rationalism, Platonism, and God*, and *Deflationism and Paradox*, but this only raises the question of who the hell is reading these books?

Digby makes a note to ask Madeleine exactly what *Cogito's* circulation amounts to and what ads cost, two questions that he saw no need to ask before he accepted the job. That was undoubtedly a wise decision.

At one o'clock, Digby decides to whip upstairs for lunch. Unfortunately, this necessitates walking through the offices of Goldenfield and MacLane, so he carries along a copy of *Cogito* and keeps it pressed close to his nose for the trip. He makes himself a cup of instant ramen soup that someone had stocked in his larder, slurps it down, and then stretches out on his featherbed for a postprandial snooze.

It is pitch black outside when Digby awakes. For a moment, he is sure he is back on Asim's couch, sleeping off a particularly stressful episode of the *Jerry Springer Show*. Instinctively, he reaches for the roach under what would be Asim's couch and in the process rolls off his bed. This awakens him completely. When he realizes where and when he is, he experiences a small trill of hysteria: he has slept through one half of his first day on the job. He attempts to calm himself by saying "But I am the boss" a few times out loud. This gets him on his feet and, moments later, down the stairs and out onto Brigham Street, Louden's main drag. He is the only person afoot.

By golly, the air is uncommonly fresh up here in the foothills of the Green Mountains. Fragrant too—newly mown grass, dewberries, and crocuses combining in an invigorating April perfume. That and the clear, star-spangled sky make him feel uncommonly fresh himself, a feeling he barely recognizes. For the first time in a very long while, he deeply inhales nothing but clean air.

Brigham Street bows around the south end of the campus where rambling, white clapboard New England homes give way to college shops, restaurants, cafés, and bars. The only one of these with a neon sign is called Louden Clear—a promising signage—so he crosses the street and enters. The place reeks with convivial chatter, but in his present perfumed mood Digby thinks he can tolerate it. He makes for the bar.

The bartender is uncommon too, a sloe-eyed Eurasian beauty in her early thirties who appears as out of place as he feels.

"Beer?" she asks.

"And something to eat," Digby replies. "I feel the need for some protein."

"Land or sea?"

"A recently killed four-legged animal would be nice."

She offers Digby the barest hint of a smile and he realizes that, like comely bartenders everywhere, she has learned to balance professional friendliness with a subtext of "Don't even think you have a chance with me." Fair enough. Digby chooses an apple-stuffed pork chop and mashed potatoes. The beer is local, a brew called Trout River, tart and bubbly as its name. He sips. He looks around the place.

The clientele, for the most part, are Louden students and they have what Digby's mother approvingly calls "fresh-scrubbed" faces. His mother means by this, among other things, *white* faces, and that they are, pinkishly white and wide-eyed. Before Digby Googled Louden College, he had no idea that student bodies like this still existed anywhere in the U.S., let alone in the Northeast. Like many small, old New England colleges, it was founded by a minister with magniloquent ideals that he was called to instill in young Christian men. Actually, this made Louden little different from, say, Amherst or Middlebury, but over the decades, while those two colleges paddled into changing currents in American thought, not to mention America's changing demographics, Louden proudly clung to Pastor Jeremiah Louden's values, among these being his high regard for light-hued skin. Not coincidentally, the intellectual quality of its student body steadily declined although, in the past several years, it experienced a modest upturn in that regard as a result of the trickle-down effect of A- and B-level colleges becoming more selective.

Two tables in the far corner are occupied by men and women in Digby's age group. It is hard to tell from the way they are dressed and coiffed whether they are connected to the college. His only clue that they might be is the expressions on their faces—they look grim.

But what is this? One of them is waving in his direction. He does the obligatory glance behind him to see if the wave's intended recipient is someone more deserving, but no, he is definitely being waved at by a fortyish blonde. Was she once one of the pretty young things with whom he had his way when he was in his early shithead years? Is she going to slap him on the shoulder and tell him that she always thought he would end his days in an obscure college town?

She is coming toward Digby and he now realizes she was the server at Mrs. Hastings' shindig.

"Max?" she says, extending a pale hand.

"Digby," he replies. "Digby Maxwell. Thanks for the croquettes."

"I defrosted them myself," she says. "I'm Winny. Would you like to join us?"

"I, uh, I just ordered my dinner."

"I'm sure Ada will be able to find you," Winny says. "Unless you'd rather be alone with your thoughts, of course."

Actually, he was about to beg off, but hearing the words "alone with your thoughts" forces him to reconsider: the thoughts he has been alone with lately have been lacking in consolation.

Winny leads the way to the corner table where he is introduced to a dour-looking, forty-something woman named Florence and a smug-looking, ponytailed fellow in his fifties named Milton. All three are Louden faculty: Florence an assistant professor of macroeconomics, Milton a full professor of applied physics, and Digby's erstwhile croquette server an instructor in creative writing who supplements her income with a small catering business. Digby has little doubt that like most faculty at middling colleges, the teachers at Louden are overqualified in their fields and under-stimulated by their students, but his sense is that they have one sweet deal here, cushy schedules and perfumed mountain air for starters, so he feels no desire to waste any compassion on them. All of these three know who he is, what brought him here and, apparently, then some.

"I was just telling them what a breath of fresh air you were last night," Winny says.

"Steamy air," Digby replies.

"Oh, that was part of your charm," Winny says.

"What *were* you doing in there—your laundry?" Milton says.

Jesus Christ, the public fishbowl of small town life. Were they going to weigh in on his bowel habits next?

Close, actually.

"I understand you're doing an issue about heaven," Florence says.

Digby's pork chop arrives and he saws off a bite before responding, simply, "Yup."

" 'Hebben, hebben, Goin' to walk all over God's hebben,' " Milton croons in what he apparently believes is African-American dialect. He wears the familiar, self-satisfied expression of an intellectual verbally slumming it. Digby wishes to God he had remained at the bar.

"I think it's a terrific idea," Winny chimes. "And so does Felicia—Mrs. Hastings."

To Digby's surprise, he finds this news exceedingly uplifting. He is not yet fully accustomed to the idea that he really does want to keep his job. Nonetheless, he restrains himself from asking for any details about Felicia's reaction. Florence asks him what he thinks of Louden so far.

"Very pretty," he says. "And very white."

"We have one heck of a time attracting African-American applicants," Florence replies earnestly.

"It would probably help if we had better than a Division Three basketball team," Milton says.

Digby experiences the fleeting desire to press Milton's face into his mashed potatoes. Actually, his desire isn't fleeting, just his will to do the deed. His restraint is aided by the fact that Winny, apparently sensing Digby's discomfort, comforts his thigh under the table. It is just a little squeeze, but it is more than enough to replace his flow of venom with a surge of libido.

Digby orders drinks all around, then sips Trout River contentedly while Scott and Florence discuss an upcoming budget meeting with Louden's president, Miles "Kim" Herker. Some sophomoric quips are knowingly exchanged concerning President Herker's ability to add and subtract. Digby passes the time by gazing at Winny.

Her hair is obviously dyed, her eyebrows plucked and painted, her impressive bosom remolded by undergarments, and a few irregularities in her skin are smoothed over with emollients, but her pale blue eyes are naked—as eyes will be—and they speak to him. They say, "Spring is in the air"; they also say, "How many springs do we have left anyhow?" Digby knows whereof her eyes speak. He squeezes her thigh by way of response. Squeeze, squeeze and an understanding is reached with nary a word spoken, a contract between primates.

They wait a discreet interval, then excuse themselves from their tablemates. Before they leave, Milton looks up at Digby and simpers, "Well, thanks to you, they may get their hands on the Hastings Towers after all."

Digby does not have the slightest idea what he is talking about.

Very little is said as Digby and Winny wend their way from Louden Clear to Winny's room in faculty housing. They both know what is up, and they both are old enough to know that even the most casual of words could cause one or the other of them to reevaluate the agenda.

CHAPTER 4

Digby's midlife dip into the world of philosophy revealed a surprising insight into his personal history: his mother, Cynthia-Marie Maxwell, was a metaphysician. She was as comfortable with the cosmic point of view as Hegel or Schopenhauer or, for that matter, Jesus. Remarkably, she was capable of surveying Being and Time from this pinnacle of abstraction even as in the physical world the highest altitude to which she ever ascended was Rock Pear Mountain, a weekend adventure sponsored by Digby's father who she always maintained was the cause of her lifelong battle with hypertension.

One of the basic tenets of Cynthia-Marie's metaphysics was her belief in some kind of Unremitting Universal Decay. In the world she inhabited, not only did bread and fruit go bad, but so went neighborhoods, nations, years, and most people. She subscribed to the First Principle that Being itself went on the skids from the moment it began, and that along that line of decline a point is marked where all traces of good are gone for good.

This, of course, raises the question of when, exactly, did Digby go bad?

He traces his skid back to his First Communion when, much to everyone's surprise—including Digby's own—the devil took up residency in his immortal soul. (In retrospect, Digby realizes that Satan had been inspired by their shared sneak viewing of Exorcist II at Passaic's Central Theatre the day before.) Preparing for the ceremony was simple: get a new suit, shirt, tie, and haircut; memorize the Hail Mary; and return to a state of grace through the Sacrament of Penance—that is, Digby's first confession. Note that Digby was only seven years old at the time and, although he had a mad crush on Debbie Epstein of the adorable, shoulder-length raven curls who sat next to him in school, he was still free from naughty thoughts, unless kakie-doodie nursery rhymes count.

Mrs. Maxwell led her only child to the confessional, straightening his tie and kissing his forehead before he made his entrance and sat down. Digby can still recall that there were tears in his eyes, tears of generalized Catholic guilt. He had rehearsed his recitation and it featured the sin of wishing his father would go away on a very long trip leaving him alone with his mother, and the time he lied to Debbie Epstein when he told her he was Jimmy Carter's nephew. Through the confessional screen, Father Bob absolved Digby of these transgressions on the spot and then asked if that was all. That is when Satan grabbed the mike. He had a high-pitched, scratchy voice.

"I have come to spawn demons," he said.

"Digby?"

"The Church will tremble, its walls will crumble." Digby-qua-Satan had apparently adapted this last bit from a graham cracker ad that was then playing on afternoon TV.

"Digby, are you all right?" Father Bob's face was flush with the screen.

"I am the anti-Christ," Digby's inner Satan concluded.

Bad. Digby had gone bad. And his first defense, that the devil made him do it, didn't ring any bells for anyone, least of all his mother. In truth, Digby pretty much believed that explanation himself. "Spawn demons?" "The anti-Christ?" These could hardly be words found in the vocabulary of a seven-year-old boy from New Jersey, precocious as he was. (Digby was as yet unaware of his uncanny ability to recall whole sections of dialogue from movies he had only seen once.)

But here is the *way* bad part. Digby got a tremendous hoot out of the whole deal. He felt rescued from the banality of his young life by his impromptu *coup de theatre*. This manifested itself in the goofy smirk which no amount of seven-year-old self-discipline could remove from his lips; it perched there for days afterward. Interestingly, Digby was nonetheless permitted to go through with his First Communion without a hitch. This undoubtedly speaks more about Father Bob's inability to alter plans—Digby's name was already printed in the Sunday program—than about the Church's benevolence.

And then it was all over. The incident was blanked out of the Maxwell household history in a matter of weeks, never to be spoken of again. Indeed, Digby had more or less forgotten about it himself until some sixteen years later when he was in psychotherapy with Dr. Epstein (no relation to Debbie). Occasioning his therapy was the fact that in less than a year after graduating college, Digby had managed to be fired by his first two employers. Both had the same complaint: Digby exhibited a patronizing attitude toward his job and, as a result, his performance of even the simplest tasks the jobs required (filing letters at the William Morris Agency, in the first instance; answering the phone and jotting down messages at a veterinarian's office in the second) was found wanting.

Dr. Epstein was enthralled by the tale of Digby's boyhood satanic attack. He declared that it was undoubtedly the key to Digby's personality. (Epstein had an extremely broad mind for a therapist. He said that the notion of the devil taking possession of Digby's soul was as plausible as any theory—say, Freud's theory about unconscious impulses—but that the devil hypothesis didn't provide them with much to talk about in their sessions, so they would stick with Freud. This places Epstein in the underpopulated camp of Utilitarian headshrinkers.)

But back to the key to Digby's personality, a subject for which Digby has a shameless interest. Epstein believed that Digby had an extreme form of reaction formation, the mechanism whereby the ego reacts to the impulses of the id by creating an antithetical formation that blocks repressed desires. To wit: in Digby's deepest self, he actually took things way *too* seriously—unbearably seriously, in fact—so he reacted with over-the-top nonchalance, also known as being a wiseass. (For those keeping track, a wiseass is a precursor of a shithead.) In any event, Epstein's analysis put a new spin on Mrs. Maxwell's metaphysics: Digby had gone bad as a reaction to his innate goodness.

Of course, Digby couldn't have been more pleased with this theory.

Later on, armed with this stunning insight, he proceeded to spend some twenty years employing his reaction formation to become a highly successful professional wiseass, namely a New York writer and editor.

He has been waiting on his deepest self's innate goodness ever since.

CHAPTER 5

"Holy cow, I thought you were dead, Digby. Or joined a cult in New Mexico."

Digby has just phoned Tommy Gasparini from his *Cogito* office. It is early in the day for him to be upright anywhere, but he has already left Winny's bed, downed a hearty breakfast at the college coffee shop, Uncommon Grounds, and changed into fresh duds. He feels post-coitally peppy and forward-looking.

"Are you saying that you miss me, Tommy?"

"Let's just say I noticed you weren't around lately."

Tommy Gasparini lives with his mother in her Bensonhurst apartment, sleeping in the same bedroom for all of his thirty-six years. By most standards, he would be considered a textbook case of arrested development, but Tommy has parlayed his sluggish maturation into minor stardom. He knows more about the comic strip universe than any other living human being of any age. True, his prose rambles and is given to gee-whizisms befitting a teenager, but his encyclopedic knowledge and preternatural insights into how comics reflect cultural currents are well worth the wholesale editing that his books and articles require. He once even made the *Times* extended best-seller list with a book about Robin, Batman's pixie sidekick, and the homoerotic undertones of that relationship. In his power days at *New York Magazine*, Digby often tapped Tommy for a piece. He is now asking him to contribute to his debut issue of *Cogito* with an illustrated article about heaven's portrayal in the comics.

"What does it pay?" Tommy asks.

"It's a prestige thing, Tommy."

"What does it pay? I'm a professional, you know."

"The mid two figures," Digby replies, then whispers, "plus sexual favors."

Tommy, of course, is not quite ready for *de facto* sex, but like most adolescents he likes dirty talk. He is chortling now.

"It would mean a lot to me, Tommy," Digby goes on. "You're the first writer I called."

After a long pause, Tommy says, "Well, I suppose I could, you know, squeeze it in," and then breaks into hiccuppy laughter at his unintended *double entendre*.

"Fifteen hundred words," Digby says.

"I didn't say that I *would* do it, just that I could."

"I'm begging you, Tommy."

"Okay. But just this once, Digby."

"You are a prince," Digby says and hangs up before Tommy can change his mind.

Zippidy, zip. It is not even ten o'clock and Digby is already making things happen. No loser, he. Digby is back in the saddle. Like all experienced garden-variety, low-grade manic-depressives, he decides to take care of some depression-postponed business while he is still riding high. He finds his daughter Sylvia's cell phone number on his own cell and presses dial. It rings a dozen times before she picks up.

"Dad?"

"It is I."

"Jesus, it's seven here, Dad. Why don't you wait another six months and call me at a decent hour."

"I'm sorry, hon. I'll call back later."

"Hey, I'm up now, you know? So what's up with you? Mom says you finally found a job."

Digby flinches, as they say, inwardly. His early morning surge of self-worth does not appear as durable as he had thought.

"Yup. It's not bad, actually. At least judging by my first day on the job. I'm up in Vermont. Small town. I'm trying to acquire simple tastes."

"Milkmaids? Trailer trash?" Sylvia says.

Digby definitely had not given enough forethought to this conversation.

"How's school, Sylvie?"

This is greeted by ironic laughter of a style that is unfamiliar to Digby, possibly a California inflection. After a few seconds, she says, "You *are* out of the loop, aren't you? I quit school four months ago."

Indeed, this *is* news to Digby, especially considering that he has been sending monthly tuition checks from his overextended American Express account to Sylvia's mother for the last year.

"Transferring to another school?"

"Way too busy for that."

"Really?"

"I guess nobody told you about *The Unmade Bed*."

Digby does not have the slightest idea what his daughter is talking about, but it seems a distinct possibility that she is a chip off the old man's block of Buenos Aires Red.

"It's an online novel, Dad," Sylvie goes on in the overly patient tone of a special needs teacher. "Like it only gets four hundred thousand hits a day."

"And you wrote it."

"Yes. Well, me and Tyler."

"Your boyfriend?"

"One of them. We alternate chapters."

"Well, how about that!" Digby says, as if he knows what he is feeling. Fatherly pride? Wonder? Inconsolable alienation from his only child?

"It's a hoot, all right."

"Terrific, hon. So Mom sends you money?"

There is a soft rap at Digby's open office door. Goldenfield and MacLane stand just outside it, whispering to each other.

"I don't need money," Sylvia is saying. "We have a sponsor."

Digby raises a finger in Goldenfield and MacLane's direction, signaling that he will be with them in a minute.

"A sponsor for this, uh . . . for *The Unmade Bed?*"

"Tyler's dad fixed it up. We carry an ad for Durex. You know, condoms. Very cute. I'll email you the site."

For the first time in over a year, Digby finds himself fully appreciating Scott Kravitz's verdict that his aptitude for spotting the very next thing plopped toiletward some time ago. An online novel that sounds vaguely smutty? And one that makes money? Not in Digby's wildest prognostications.

Abruptly and without fully realizing it, Digby momentarily slips into the head of an aging curmudgeon from which he sees nothing but rampant idiocy in the coming generation's *modem operandi.* But in a beat he returns to his aspiring-to-remain-youthful self and says, "That's just terrific, Sylvie. I can't wait to see it."

"You want to hang up now, am I right?" Sylvie says.

Obviously, her aptitude for pressing her father's guilt button has continued to flourish.

"Not really," Digby replies.

"Whatever. I know your wind-up voice," Sylvia says. "Bye, Digby."

Although Digby's curmudgeonly lapse was silent, Sylvia immediately picked up on it, 'rampant idiocy' and all. She has her own version of her father's talent for empathy: she hears personal criticisms where others hear nothing at all. And she hears them often. Her reflexive brashness, even her dirty mouth, fools few of her friends and only rarely herself. When she hangs up the phone in her Berkeley apartment, she tries to find and assume the exact position in which she had been sleeping when her father called, but it eludes her. "God damn him," she says out loud.

"Bye, Sylvia," Digby says, although he already hears the drone of the dial tone, a sound that fleetingly reminds him of the monotony of parental failure.

Goldenfield and MacLane take these parting words as a cue to enter his office and stand directly in front of his desk.

"My daughter," Digby says to them. For some reason, these words come out of his mouth sounding like a pathetic excuse, possibly even a lie, but in any event neither of the duo looking down at him seems to take an interest. They appear to have weightier matters on their minds. "What's up?" Digby says.

"We're running into a little—" Goldenfield begins.

"Reticence," MacLane finishes.

Digby cannot suppress a grin. The pair seems like comic strip twins who scheme with a single diabolical mind, except that it is hard to imagine these two having shared anybody's womb.

"From whom?" Digby asks.

"Our regular contributors, for starters," Goldenfield manages to say all on his own.

"Not up for heaven, are they?" Digby says, gratefully back in full ironic mode.

"More than that, they feel that the subject is, well, undignified," MacLane says.

"Oh, the dignity thing," Digby goes on raffishly. His inner child is hooting, *"Nah, nah, Mommy Felicia likes my idea, so there!"* He hadn't realized until now how very much Mrs. Hastings' reported approval has bucked him up, and Digby tends toward raffishness when bucked up.

"Maybe we should consider some kind of compromise," Goldenfield says.

"Please do sit down," Digby says. "My neck isn't what it used to be."

They sit on the Victorian settee. For a fleeting moment, Digby thinks they look kind of adorable there.

"There are a lot of interesting ideas in the literature about the soul," Goldenfield goes on. "As in, 'the immortal soul.' Aristotle's 'psyche' is a good place to start."

"And then we could insert the biblical soul that supposedly goes to heaven in one of our articles, if you see what I mean," MacLane says.

"Just for fun," Digby says.

"Well, yes, for a little bit of fun," Goldenfield says tentatively.

"But not too much fun," Digby says.

The two of them eye Digby warily. It is very astute of them to do so.

"I imagine that for the two of you, fun is the opposite of serious," Digby says with all the seeming seriousness he can muster. "You can't hold both concepts in your mind at the same time."

All traces of adorableness have evaporated from their faces.

"Actually I do think you two are on to something," Digby goes on. "We definitely should do a piece about souls, especially of the immortal variety. And if Aristotle is a good springboard, hey, go for it. But get that soul to heaven, you hear? The Great Hereafter. Sweet Beulah Land. Because that's what our next issue is about!"

No response. No movement to leave either. Finally MacLane says, "There's something else. Duke University Press."

This, Digby recalls, is the publisher who rents the back page of *Cogito* to promote philosophy books with inscrutable titles.

"What about them?" Digby asks. He sniffs that foul, gassy odor again.

"They are not happy with the topic," Goldenfield says.

Digby is on his feet in an instant. He shouts, "And who the fuck told them what our topic is? They're advertisers, not contributors! It's none of their fucking business!"

Goldenfield and MacLane appear frightened. Digby finds this encouraging.

"I simply happened to be on the phone with Raymond Bates—" Goldenfield begins, but Digby has had enough.

"Get the hell out of here!" he shouts, and they do.

Digby feels both energized and shaky. Actually, he could use a quick toke, but to his credit, he merely sits down and tries to calm himself, not an easy task considering that he doesn't know what his options are—for example, is he allowed to fire these two for insubordination? Or, on the other hand, can they fuck him over with just a few well-placed phone calls?

Digby's management skills are not what they used to be—and they never were, as Fanny used to quip. He reaches back to his months in front of Asim's television set and asks himself, what would Donald Trump do? But before an answer comes, Madeleine calls to him from the door, "Have you seen Rostislav?"

"No."

"He seems to be missing," Madeleine says anxiously.

"Missing? From where?"

"I don't know. Everywhere, I guess. He didn't show up for his seminar. He's not in his room. He's not here either."

"That doesn't seem like an awful lot of places not to be," Digby says. "Not enough to qualify as missing. He's a grown man. Maybe he's sleeping in at a girlfriend's house."

"He doesn't have a girlfriend," Madeleine replies peevishly.

Fishbowl that Louden, Vermont is, minnows of Madeleine's past have swum into Digby's view these past few days. She is the daughter of a deceased classics professor and a logger's widow to whom he may or may not have been married. Madeleine has a daughter of her own; although no one seems to know for sure who the father is, several past and present humanities instructors are the prime suspects. Nonetheless, Madeleine seems the very opposite of a desperate woman. In New York, she would be deemed a 'highly centered' person, the highest compliment of the New Age set.

"I see," Digby says. He needs to get back to more pressing matters, like the guerilla rebellion of fifty percent of his staff.

"Rosti is terribly absentminded," Madeleine goes on. "I'm afraid it can be a problem for him."

"Yes, well, I'm sure it will work out," Digby says, deliberately booting up his computer in a way that is supposed to communicate: *Please go away.* But it does not so communicate. Madeleine continues: "Sometimes, working on a computation in his head, Rosti can forget—"

"Madeleine, I need to make a call now," Digby says. This is a verbal tactic he learned watching the characters on General Hospital passive-aggressively manipulate one another. He wonders how many people pick up tips for efficient social maneuvers by watching the soaps—there is probably an article in there somewhere.

Indeed, Madeleine withdraws just as Digby's Mac flashes on with the message that he has email from Sylvia. He clicks. "Check it out, Dad" is Sylvie's message. Digby is encouraged by the fact that she has addressed him as 'Dad' and not 'Biological Father,' the appellation she assigned him for several months following his divorce from her mother. He clicks on the link. Up pops the home page of *The Unmade Bed—an interactive novel in progress, by Sylvia Maxwell and Tyler Flynn.*

The graphics are dazzling. First, an establishment shot of a tasteful brass double bed that would have made the Hastings' decorator proud. Then, in live motion, a young man approaches the bed in his underwear. Suddenly, everything accelerates to Keystone Cops speed as a young woman in bra and panties appears on the other side of the bed, they both slip out of their undies, dive into bed, engage in athletic sex, and then the guy jumps out of bed only to be immediately replaced by another guy who sheds his underwear.

It is at this point that Digby abruptly clicks to the next page. Not only does he get the concept, but he has the excruciating suspicion that in slower motion he might identify the young woman as his daughter. Yet the next page brings little solace: it is the sponsor's ad page. An animated inflated condom bearing a smiley face is poised on two spindly legs that end in outsized sneakers. He stands on the sidewalk in a pleasant urban neighborhood, peering around and scratching his head. He then dives into a sewer pipe, but quickly emerges, shaking his head. *No, that's not what I wanted to get into.* He then dives into a mail slot, but once again emerges disappointed. Now he spots a sexy, miniskirted woman coming toward him. *Yup, now I'm in business.*

Digby quickly clicks again, and *The Unmade Bed* begins in earnest:

> *Chapter One:*
>
> *Sex is like food—if you are served the same meal every day, after a while you become anorexic. That meal, no matter how well prepared, is missing that spice known as variety . . .*

Digby sighs—*Oh dear, my daughter, the writer.* He does not feel good about his parenting. He has a sudden, nightmarish suspicion: *he* is her role model. The phone rings and he snaps up the receiver, eager for distraction.

"We need to talk," Felicia Hastings says curtly by way of greeting.

"My thought exactly," Digby replies.

"Louden Clear in fifteen minutes," she says and hangs up.

It could have been the terse dialogue of a pair of illicit lovers, only decidedly more ominous. By tone of voice alone, Digby is convinced that his days at *Cogito* are already dwindling down to a precious few. He sees his featherbed taking flight without him. He feels a tingle of nostalgia for his three days in Louden, Vermont. How sweet they were! How fresh and enchanting! Those were the good old days.

He rises from his leather-cushioned chair and is off, passing through Goldenfield's and MacLane's unoccupied offices—no doubt they took off for Felicia's manse directly after his colloquy with them. He flies past Madeleine, deep in a tense telephone conversation about the missing logician, and on to sunny Brigham Street.

Oh yes, bethinks Digby, I am going to miss this colonial village and its gaggles of pastel sweater-wearing coeds. Pink, tangerine, tawny—tones that on a cashmere sweater worn by a young woman seem another delicious layer of skin.

But these pastel thoughts are abruptly arrested as someone taps Digby on the shoulder from behind. He turns. It is none other than last night's bedmate sporting a sexy smile, or at least Digby guesses that Winny intends her smile to be sexy, but to his eye it looks a bit loopy. That the layer of foundation on her face absorbs the bright morning sunlight like a black hole does not help the effect.

"I'm in a bit of a hurry," Digby says. "Big meeting with the boss."

"Kiss for luck," Winny replies, and before Digby can reply she is planting a moist smooch on his lips, complete with some tricky tongue work. He backs away as soon as he politely can, making little bows like an altar boy respectfully fleeing the embrace of a priest.

"Gotta run," he says.

"Encore tonight?" Winny calls after him.

Although last night's coupling had been extremely gratifying— earthy and bouncy with both growls and giggles aplenty— Digby is apprehensive about scheduling a repeat performance so soon. For starters, he just arrived here and he knows how easily he falls into regular habits. He makes a sound somewhere between "uh, *huh*" and "*uh*, uh" and breaks into a trot all the way to the restaurant.

Felicia Hastings is waiting for Digby at the same table at which he made new friends last night. She is wearing a surprisingly stylish, robin's-egg blue blazer and a long black skirt, perhaps a transitional get-up from the widow's weeds she had been sporting since he first met her at the Harvard Club. She says, "Sit down, Mr. Maxwell."

Digby does as told.

"Is it too early for a drink?" she asks.

Digby winces. *Jesus, it's going to be that bad, eh?*

"Not too early for me," Digby replies. "A Bloody Mary— just for the vitamins, of course."

Felicia calls to the barman for two Bloody Marys, then waits silently for them to be served. Digby takes this opportunity to study her face for clues to his fate. Remarkably, he had not noticed before that she has bright green eyes that at this moment seem to sparkle like a woman still in her sexual prime. Or is it that between *The Unmade Bed* and the bevy of pastel sweaters on Brigham Street—not to mention Winny's tongue work—he sees sexual innuendo in everything? The drinks arrive. Felicia raises her glass to Digby's.

"To heaven," she says, winking.

"My favorite destination," he replies, clinking her glass. *By God, maybe it isn't time for Louden nostalgia yet, after all.*

Felicia takes a dainty sip of her drink and says, "Excuse my language, but Elliot Goldenfield has his head up his rectum."

Digby giggles. It is an involuntary reaction.

"And that MacLane woman or man or whatever she thinks she is this week, she is no more a philosopher than Rush Limbaugh," Felicia goes on. "The fact is Bonner only brought her on board under pressure from the department head. Bonner always said that gender studies is the last refuge of women who cannot fathom linear thought."

Digby's head is spinning. Clearly, he has underestimated Felicia Hastings' intellectual sparkle too.

"They certainly aren't happy with the new direction we're taking," he says.

"No, no, they made that very clear to me," Felicia says, more seriously now. "I'd like to just cut them loose, but that might be more trouble than it's worth. Too much fuss. Too much campus chatter. But I have an idea for how to deal with them."

"I'm all ears."

"You assign them a dissent column. Let them rail all they want about how dumb it is to discuss heaven in a philosophy magazine. How undignified, blah, blah. That should keep them satisfied. It'll also give them ample opportunity to look like the stodgy idiots they are."

"I do like the way you think, Mrs. Hastings," he responds.

"Thank you, Digby. But it's not my idea, it's Bonner's."

"Beg pardon?"

"I spoke with him right after those two left the house," Felicia says, smiling merrily. "He was angry, and when Bonner is angry he comes up with his best ideas."

At this point, Digby is far from considering himself anything even close to a philosopher, but nonetheless he generally comes down on the side of rational thought, so Felicia's blithe reference to chatting with her late husband gives him pause. Why this should give him pause while an issue of an academic philosophy journal devoted to Divine Lalaland does not, he is unready to consider.

"I'll give them the assignment as soon as I see them," he replies, but Felicia is no longer looking at him. She has half-risen from her chair and is waving enthusiastically to a woman who has just stepped into the entrance of Louden Clear. This woman, shortish and mid-thirtyish, with close-cut dirty blonde hair, immediately heads for their table. She has an elegant smile and appears uncommonly grounded.

"Mary, you're right on time," Felicia says. "This is Mr. Maxwell, our new editor. Digby, this is Mary Bonavitacola—*Reverend* Mary Bonavitacola of our Unitarian Church."

Hands are shaken and Mary sits down next to Digby, the same seat in which Winny sat last night. Perhaps that is why he has the passing urge to pat the good reverend's thigh under the table.

"I told Mary about your heaven issue," Felicia is saying. "And I don't want to overstep here—you *are* the editor-in-chief, Digby—but Mary does have some interesting ideas about paradise. She's Swarthmore too, you know."

"I guess this is the moment when we do our secret handshake," Mary says, looking at Digby with extraordinarily radiant deep blue eyes.

Digby observes that she is not wearing a wedding ring. He asks her to marry him.

No, he doesn't, but it seems like a perfectly rational thing to do. Not only does he feel a powerful attraction to this woman, but he also senses some kind of preternatural connection to her, as if the two of them had been deep in intimate conversation untold lifetimes ago. This is total nonsense, of course; nonetheless, in the moment it seems as real to Digby as Bonner's ghost must appear to Mrs. Hastings. Perhaps it is the rarified air up here in Vermont's soaring Green Mountains.

"Paul Tillich had some interesting ideas about eternity," Mary says. "Eternal life in the here and now. 'The eternal now,' he called it."

"But no trumpets and golden temples, I gather," Digby says, trying to look thoughtful and smart.

"Not unless you happen to be at a Wynton Marsalis concert at the Taj Mahal at that eternal moment," Mary quips.

Digby wonders if Mary is too old to bear children. His.

"Twenty-five hundred words by May first," he says to Mary.

"Thank you, but maybe you should hear what I have in mind first," the reverend replies. "Like at my sermon this Sunday."

Digby does not immediately reply because he is momentarily distracted by a figure passing outside Louden Clear's windows. It is Rosti, the logician, and he does seem deep in thought; in fact, he is jabbering to himself whilst poking at the air with his right index finger. Digby considers rushing outside and—what? Collaring him? Ordering him to turn himself in to Madeleine? And by virtue of this interruption missing even a few seconds of sitting next to Reverend Bonavitacola? Not a chance.

"I am not a good hymn singer," Digby replies.

"Mouth the words," she says, smiling and standing.

Don't go!

She goes.

"I need to nap," Mrs. Hastings says as she prepares to leave. "I think that went well, don't you?"

"Yes," Digby says. "By the way, Felicia, what's this gossip about somebody trying to get his hands on Hastings Towers?"

Felicia smiles and exits too, leaving Digby to pay the bill.

CHAPTER 6

For church, Digby wears his magazine-awards-dinner tan suit complete with a black silk tie which gives him the appearance of a South American mayor on the Day of the Dead. The few times he has been to church in the past thirty years have been solely for funerals and weddings, including his own wedding. Undoubtedly, someone put in charge of such things will outfit him in this very same suit for his funeral, at a church or otherwise.

Louden's Universalist Unitarian Church is housed in a close-to-the-road, red brick building that clearly served some other function not too long ago; extrapolating from its clunky, foursquare appearance, that function was as a five-and-dime store before it went the way of all such stores when malls K-marted them up to five-and-dime heaven. The edifice still has its original display windows on either side of the entrance, both crowded with upstanding books on social problems like African starvation and AIDS, plus assorted posters advertising local lectures and meetings, most of these devoted to heart-breaking social problems too. The only sign of cheeriness is a hand-lettered poster that names Mary Bonavitacola as the pastor in residence and her sermon topic for today: "**Heaven— Been There, Done That.**"

Digby makes his way inside and takes a seat in the last pew, although it is far too plushy to qualify as a genuine, New England pew; Digby's guess is that the chairs were purchased at the liquidation sale of a bankrupt funeral parlor.

Just as Digby sits down, a bearded young man appears at the altar, guitar in hand and neck-braced harmonica in mouth, and begins playing, "Sweet Beulah Land." His rendition, like Unitarianism itself, wavers between the gritty and the wry. Some congregants start singing and swaying. Digby mouths the words.

Clearly, Digby is overdressed for this group of worshippers. Not a suit coat or tie in sight. Instead, work shirts, cardigan sweaters, jeans, and, at least in his row, a good number of heavy work boots, some on strapping young women. The music man moves on to the hymn, "Count Your Blessings," and Digby finds himself drifting off as he tries to conjure thoughts of gratitude.

Actually, he *is* feeling surprisingly grateful these last few days. He is experiencing a form of contentment that until recently he believed was lost to him forever—job security. With Bonner Hastings' otherworldly help, he has quelled the Goldenfield-MacLane insurrection; those two are busy as drones working on their indignant dissent column. Digby often hears them laughing derisively in their offices when, it would appear, they fashion a particularly snarky sentence attacking him and his heaven. Plus, Digby's relationship with his daughter has taken a pleasant upturn, even if it is founded on his somewhat disingenuous enthusiasm for her interactive smut-lit. And then there is Mary . . . but alas, Digby's blessings-counting reverie is abruptly interrupted by a warm hand that has landed in his lap.

It should be noted here that the mix of religion and sex has always had a strong appeal to Digby. Like most forced-to-attend-church adolescents, he experienced his share of erotic fantasies involving horny nuns and nubile young choirgirls naked under their robes. Furthermore, before he even snaps open his eyes, he knows that the hand frolicking in his lap belongs to Winny, she of the robust sexual appetite. Nonetheless the entire maneuver strikes him as sacrilegious. Yes indeed, he feels a buzz of righteous indignation as he lifts off her fingers. *Terrific feeling, righteous indignation. No wonder entire political movements have been built upon it.*

Of course, Digby's real reason for distancing Winny's fingers from his midsection is that he has come to church this Sunday not only to evaluate Mary Bonavitacola's sermon for its possible inclusion in *Cogito*, but to gaze upon the reverend's remarkable blue eyes, eyes that—not to put too fine a point on it—seem to offer him a finer life. The very notion of a finer life is new to Digby; he usually sees all lives as more or less equal in the sense that in the end they all add up to the same sum—namely naught. 'Being' swiftly followed by 'Nothingness.' And even in these recent days when he sensed that maybe there just might be something out there that could furnish him with a better, more meaningful life, he was convinced that he did not deserve it—or, certainly, did not deserve *her.* Nonetheless, for this remote possibility alone, Digby is certain that a fondle job in the rearmost pew of the Louden Universalist Unitarian Church does not seem like a good idea.

"Why Miss Winifred, I didn't know you were a God-fearing creature too," he whispers to his pewmate by way of apology for the finger removal.

"Oh, I'm not," she whispers back. "I'm just here to stalk you."

Digby fears there is truth in her jest.

Mary appears onstage in an unflattering, floral-patterned linen dress, and proceeds to read a verse from the Good Book, but this being a Unitarian Church, that good book is Eckhart Tolle's *The Power of Now.*

Digby clenches his teeth. *Dear me, have I misjudged Ms. Bonavitacola? Is she a New Age Airhead in flax clothing?*

" 'I was gripped by an intense fear, and my body started to shake,' " Reverend Mary reads. " 'I could feel myself being sucked into a void. It felt as if the void was inside myself rather than outside. Suddenly, there was no more fear, and I let myself fall into that void.' "

Digby has more than a passing acquaintance with the void within; it is the one he has been trying to suffuse with marijuana smoke the past year or so. Mary closes the book and sets it down on her lectern. She smiles out at her flock. Digby smiles back sheepishly. *Does she see me? Would it be inappropriate for me to wave?*

"Usually, Eckhart Tolle gives me the fantods," Mary continues. "A little too 'golly gee' for my taste. But that particular passage kind of knocked me out because I've had a few run-ins with the Big Void myself. Especially after Reuben died."

Reuben?

"Her husband," Winny whispers, reading Digby's perplexed expression.

"People say that when a loved one dies, he remains alive in your heart," Mary goes on. "But what they are reluctant to tell you is that part of yourself dies with your loved one. It leaves a void. And that void never goes away. *Never.*"

Here and there in the converted five-and-dime Digby hears muted sniffles. Mary acknowledges these with a respectful pause, but her resolute gaze is a peremptory warning against pity, for her or for oneself.

"It's a battle," she goes on. "Me against the void. A battle to the death. If the void takes over my life, I'm done for. And for a whole bunch of nothingness that void is a remarkably powerful adversary."

The reverend offers a melancholy smile, one that resonates somewhere in the area of Digby's voided soul. This resonance says to him that he has gone through much of his adult life confusing existential despair with mere discontent, mistaking angst over the meaningless of life for crankiness brought on by picayune peeves. *I am superficial to the core. And the time is nigh—very nigh—for me to have a serious talk with my inner self. Possibly even a philosophical talk.*

"Let me tell you about a moment," Reverend Mary continues, "a moment that lasted no longer than it takes to scratch your nose—but nonetheless a moment that sometimes gives me an edge on that feeling of emptiness. That is, when I truly remember that moment. When I don't simply remember that it happened, but I actually slip back into it. Live that moment again."

As a point of pride, Digby has never allowed himself to feel a part of a rapt audience. It smacks of groupthink. And for him, a church congregation is the most flagrant laboratory of groupthink in the civilized world, the kind of groupthink that usually ends in group mayhem. That said, he is listening like an acolyte to Reverend Bonavitacola.

"After his last round of chemo and the doctors giving Reuben only a few more weeks to live, we rented a small cottage out on Cape Cod. It was late fall, cold and raw, but every evening we would bundle up and sit on the wicker daybed out on the deck to watch the sunset. Just sit there and watch that ball of red slip into the sea. No words. Nothing to say, really. What can you say?"

Not so much as a rustle or murmur in the church.

"During one of those sunsets, just a few days before Reuben died, I had a peculiar thought about time itself. I saw time as a dimension that, for that particular moment, I was not a part of. It was just there by itself. Time. And I was looking at it. Very impressive thing, time. Even more impressive when, for that moment, I had the perspective of looking at it as something separate from me.

"Then another thought or feeling hit me. Right now, sitting here on the daybed with Reuben watching the sun go down, right now is eternity. Because eternity is not forever, the way I usually think of it, but eternity is being outside of time. And that's where I was for that moment. Outside of time. But completely inside now. Now. The eternal now."

Here, Mary lets loose with the most beatific smile Digby has ever seen this side of a Raphael.

"It was heaven," she says.

The congregation waits for her to go on. But that is it. End of sermon.

"For those who pray, now might be a good time to do it," Mary says, then nods to the music man to replace her at the altar. The music man obliges with a particularly sappy version of Bette Midler's "Heaven." If his intention is to break the mood, he succeeds admirably.

Digby is not one of those who pray, so he has some time on his hands. What he would really like to do is get out of here and get out by himself, but he is pretty sure that were he to make his way up the aisle, Miss Winny would follow close behind him. This is all his own doing, Digby is certain, and it is not the first time that by satisfying some free-floating lust he has implied promises that he had no desire to keep. In any other church, this would make him a sinner in God's eyes, but today God is unnecessary. Sin has got him cornered in this church's last pew.

Digby closes his eyes as the service goes on. Somebody talks about a local Habitat for Humanity project and the need for volunteers owning hammers. Digby is confident the man has come to the right place. Someone else talks about the need for condoms in Africa to stem the spread of AIDS. Digby has a fleeting vision of a plate being passed among the pews and his good neighbors dropping packets of Trojans in it. Actually, it occurs to him that Sylvia's sponsor could spread a little good will by donating a shipload of rubbers to the Africans and then having one of their smiley-faced, spindly-legged mascots boast about it on her website.

More music, a breathy medley of Sweet Honey in the Rocks classics. Another speaker, this one going on about what everyone should be doing about childhood obesity. Digby is finally able to tune it all out and think. He tries to get his mind around Mary's heaven-on-Cape Cod experience, but it keeps slipping away like the sun into the Atlantic. Still, for the first time since he was a teenager—the very embodiment of that adolescent archetype, the public wise guy cloaking a private brooder—he finds himself yearning for some kind of enlightenment. Nothing fancy, just a glimpse of the transcendental plane would do him for now. He glimpses not.

A final sing-along—some African ditty that everyone but Digby seems to know by heart—and then Digby is on his way out, thoughts of a few deep tokes dancing in his head. He is in possession of a Huxley-like intuition that what his mind needs to gather the full meaning of Mary's eternal moment is a chemical nudge. But it is not to be, at least not yet. The unmistakable voice of Felicia Hastings is calling him by name. She is waiting for him at the exit.

"So, what do you think?" Felicia asks me. "You know, as an editor."

It takes a moment for Digby to recall his original reason for coming to church.

"The eternal moment thing?" he says finally.

"For *Cogito*," Felicia says. "She said it was heaven."

"Well, yes, she did, didn't she?" Digby fumbles. "I think it's very promising. A little abstract, maybe. And I'd like to know a bit more about why she calls it heaven, you know?"

"I could have just as well called it Duluth, I suppose." It is Mary Bonavitacola's voice. She has just sidled up beside Digby and she is smiling. Digby turns and looks into her wonderful eyes. Stretching this moment for an eternity seems, at this moment, like a divine idea. Maybe he is getting the hang of this.

"That does it," Digby replies. "I am devoting the next issue of *Cogito* to Duluth."

"Did it—my sermon—make any sense?" Mary asks, sounding winningly insecure.

"Perfect sense," Digby replies. "Personally, I have always planned on living in the present."

They have a lovely laugh. Digby's, however, abruptly terminates when he sees Winny sashay up on his other side. She slips her arm through his.

"But don't you think her sermon would fit just perfectly?" Felicia is saying.

"Not fair," Mary says. "I'm sure Digby wants to think about it."

Digby! She said my name! I am a teenager in love. Sing that one, Mr. Music Man!

"Yes, I'll think about it. Then maybe we could have a talk about it," Digby says in his best professional voice. However, this voice is difficult to maintain at the same time that he is trying, with body language, to express to Winny that he would like her to give him more personal space, both geometric and spiritual.

"Why, hello, Winny," Felicia is saying. "Everybody knows each other, don't they?"

They all acknowledge that they do.

"Winny has been introducing Digby to the delights of our little town," Felicia goes on merrily, that still-in-her-sexual-prime sparkle flashing from her eyes again.

It occurs to Digby that Felicia Hastings is actually the devil. Just a passing thought, really.

"I'm late," Digby blurts. And he is off, skedaddling out the church door and trotting toward Brigham Street without so much as a toodle-oo. He knows, of course, that this is a coward's exit.

CHAPTER 7

Passing by Write Now, Brigham Street's stationery, greeting card, and newspaper shop, Digby feels a yen for sensory overload, so he dips inside and buys a copy of the Sunday *New York Times* and a jumbo bag of Cracker Jacks. Combined with an infusion of Buenos Aires Red, he figures this should keep his options open—either deep philosophical understanding or mindless vegetation—for the rest of the Lord's Day. His codeword for the day: The Void.

Only moments after Digby is out the door, he runs into Madeleine Follet, although it takes him a moment to recognize her out of *Cogito* context. She is wearing a khaki jacket dangling with binoculars and an iPhone, baggy jeans, and laced-up rubber boots that would have made her feel right at home at the Unitarian Church. Following behind her are a pair of similarly outfitted teenage girls and an elderly man, although this last has forsaken hiking gear for Bermuda shorts and a trademarked "Life is Good" sweatshirt. (Digby wonders if some enterprising college kid will trademark "Life is Bad" for the Goth set.) Digby plays it safe and says simply, "Hi there."

"We should have done this days ago," Madeleine replies grimly. "You should put on something more substantial, Digby. We may be hitting some pretty heavy terrain."

"Beg pardon?"

"Didn't you get my email? We're searching for Rosti. I figure he's in the mountains somewhere. Totally lost and becoming dehydrated."

Aha, the peripatetic logician.

"Actually, I just saw him the other day," Digby says. "He was walking along the street right here. The only lost he looked was in his thoughts."

"*When?*" Madeleine barks. "*What day?*"

"Thursday."

"Jesus, that's four days ago. Where did he say he was going?"

"He didn't. I didn't want to disturb him. He seemed on the brink of something important, possibly involving 'X's relationship to Y,' but I can't be sure."

Madeleine does not find this in the least droll.

When Digby Maxwell first arrived at Cogito, *Madeleine had found his boyish flippancy refreshing, especially in contrast to Goldenfield and MacLane's relentless self-seriousness. Although Madeleine had never in all these years heard Mr. Hastings himself say anything about wanting the magazine to become more entertaining and relevant to the general public, Maxwell certainly seemed like the perfect man for that job. Yet in only a matter of days, Madeleine has found herself becoming more irritated than amused by him. It was one thing to be clever, but it was quite another to be seemingly incapable of taking anyone seriously.*

"Look, you go ahead and I'll try to catch up to you later, okay?" Digby goes on, doing some impromptu eyebrow pumping that he hopes comes off as worried concern.

Madeleine and her troopers start to move on, but not before she quips out of the side of her mouth, "Check your email. Duke has flown the coop."

Duke? Duke Edward Kennedy Ellington, Dad's absolute favorite? Digby's mind remains a bit messy from trying to contemplate Time, the dimension. He remains standing in the same spot after Madeleine and her posse have already headed for the hills. Then it comes back to him—Duke University Press, publishers of wooly monographs and clearly *Cogito*'s main source of advertising revenue. Flying from the coop because Goldenfield and MacLane ratted out his heaven. Well, Digby thinks, Duke was probably wise to do so. Instead of selling two copies of their book, *Deflationism and Paradox*, they will now probably only sell one. But how much difference could Duke's withdrawal make to the magazine's financial picture anyhow? Felicia has made it very clear that Bonner's trust fund is what keeps *Cogito* in four-color covers and slick bond paper. The hell with them.

As Digby approaches his happy new home, he spots two middle-aged workmen on the sward of grass and wildflowers just beyond his office window. One of them is holding a clipboard, the other stands behind a transit on a tripod. Seeing Digby, they both chuckle. It occurs to Digby that perhaps he has been playing to the wrong audience in this town.

"You must be Professor Maxwell," the man behind the transit says, grinning.

"Minus the professor," Digby replies. This elicits an even heartier laugh. "What's up?"

"Just updating," the transit guy says.

"We get time and a half for working on a Sunday," his partner adds.

"Doing a survey?" Digby asks.

"Yup. Not that anything's changed in the last fifty years, but that just makes our job easier," replies Transit Man. He seems to find his own remark hilarious too. It is then that Digby observes the cap of a pint of bourbon obtruding from his pants pocket. *In bourbon hilaritas.*

"Work for the college?" Digby asks.

"Yeah, well, sort of," he replies with diminished heartiness. "The Hastings Towers thing, you know. Land lust, my old man calls it. They must have surveyed this plot a hundred times on his watch."

"Who's lusting for it?"

"The college for this dinosaur," Transit Man says, nodding toward Digby's office and abode.

"Well, what do you know?" Digby says, wondering what they know that he doesn't.

The workmen give him a weary look and go back to their work.

Digby now takes his first good look at the coveted Hastings Towers. It certainly is a fine example of Empire fantasy, constructed out of handmade crimson bricks with white wood details, a mansard roof covered with patterned shingles and punctuated with oriel windows, one of which juts out from Digby's bedroom. On its north side is a silo-sized turret with a conical roof topped with an ironwork lion growling, or possibly yawning—undoubtedly the Hastings coat of arms.

"Well, have a happy day!" Digby says, hoping to reanimate their budding friendship. "Have a happy day" is a phrase that Digby never dreamed would pass his lips unencumbered by irony.

Upstairs in his Hastings Towers digs, Digby strips off his Sunday best, pulls on his lucky silk robe, sits down at the kitchen table and rolls himself a blunt the size of a corona. He lights up. Then he grabs a handful of Cracker Jacks and pulls out the Styles section of the *Times*. He skims an article about the ubiquity of Twitter gossip—apparently Martha Stewart tweeted glowingly about her lovely lunch with Ludacris at Michael's between courses of said lunch—and turns to his favorite column, Vows. Chaitali Bopori and David Siegel were wed yesterday in an interfaith ceremony at Landmark on the Park. She wore a sari, he wore Hugo Boss, the Hindu priest sported an ersatz skullcap, and the rabbi fingered a lotus. Chaitali and David met in a chat room for Jane Austen scholars, *God bless them.*

Digby realizes that he has uttered these last three words out loud and this realization confirms for him that his Buenos Aires Red is already working its magic, so he stretches out on his featherbed. *"God bless them?"* Exactly what is the nature of this softening of his brain?

He reaches for his Bose remote and clicks on the local NPR outlet which, for the Sabbath, is airing his favorite love-to-hate program, *Hearts of Space*, an hour's worth of New Age Muzak.

Truth to tell, the repeating trills and long-held minor chords are only a gurgling waterfall away from the minimalist offerings of the sophisticates' darling, Philip Glass. A stunning observation, Digby decides. No, he is not going brain dead up here in Vermont, he is finally seeing through the Manhattan fog.

In a trice, he is at one with the trills and gurgles of *Hearts of Space* and he drifts off.

In Digby's dream, he is pacing the rim of a crater—a volcano? the moon?—and peers gingerly down into it. The thing is bottomless. If he were to tumble in, he would never hit the ground, just float downward for an eternity. And in that dream moment, that is exactly what he wants to do. What he needs to do.

But suddenly he feels nauseous. Terrified. Holy Moses, this is it! The Void! Eternal nothingness! The raven is quothing, "Nevermore!"

Dreams being inexpensive independent films, he is abruptly flashed back to his desk at *New York Magazine* where he is perusing an array of clippings and handwritten notes spread out before him. He is asking himself, What is the very next thing? His deadline is looming. He needs to make a pick. But then a whirlwind lifts the scraps into its funnel and all that is left is that crater again. *The very next thing is The Void!*

He crashes awake in a sopping sweat. An ethereal voice is calling his name. "Digby? Digby?" Jesus, his day of reckoning *has* come. He is being summoned to the other side. He sits up in his bed, banging his head against the brass bedstead. "Digby? I know you're in there."

Winny. In the instant, he is relieved that he can avoid the void, at least for now, even if, in another sense, his moment of reckoning *has* arrived.

"I'm indisposed," Digby calls weakly toward the door.

"Is somebody else in there?"

"No," he says. "Well, in a way. I'm communing with my Maker."

"You are not being nice," comes Winny's winsome reply. "I'm feeling a little, you know, lonesome."

"I know that feeling," he says. "But it does have its rewards. You get acquainted with your inner self."

"And I'm also feeling used," Winny says.

Oy, as they say in Manhattan. Judging by the clench in Digby's stomach, it appears he is not beyond feelings of mere mundane guilt. He supposes this is a good sign spiritual-wise, a suitable starting place for ascending to cosmic guilt, which clearly is only a stone's throw away from redemption. He opens the door. Winny steps in, all smiles.

"I've been lounging," Digby says, gesturing toward his newspaper-and-Cracker-Jack-strewn bed.

"Oh, is that what they call it these days?" Winny intones superciliously.

"How's that?"

"You can smell the weed all the way down to the bottom of the stairway," she says.

"Oh, that. I only use it for medical reasons."

Winny giggles. It has a surprisingly pleasant sound.

"I'm feeling a bit sickly myself, Doctor," she says.

Clearly this is Digby's cue to offer her his blunt, but he hesitates. Not out of drug covetousness, mind you; when it comes to pot, he has always been a good sharer. But because he can see where this will lead, as surely as lies lead to more lies. He does not wish to bed Miss Winifred today or, almost certainly, any future day. Call him fickle. Possibly, even call him callous. But on the other hand, it may be that his reaction time is improving; in his full-immersion shithead years, he would continue to sleep with a woman even as he read their affair's expiration date on her naked torso. He is absolutely positive that he does not want to spend any long term quality time with Winny, so this freshly minted vow of his will preemptively quash a lot of sorrow down the road for both of them. Actually, he believes he is being considerate.

In fact, Winifred's designs on Digby are far more sketchy than he presumes, proving once again that guilt-prone men usually have an exaggerated idea of their impact on women.

Not unlike the narrators of The Unmade Bed, *Winny has a variegated palate when it comes to sex and sexual partners. She has even toyed with the idea of committing some of her amatory experiences and observations to print in the form of a modern romance novel. She certainly enjoyed her little tumble with Digby and would enjoy another tumble or two with him, but her future plans go no further than that.*

"There's something I've been meaning to ask you," Digby says. "What's all the to-do about this building? Hastings Towers. I mean, apparently the college covets it."

"Are you going to offer me a toke or not?" is Winny's reply. It is a reasonable question, actually.

Digby retrieves the joint from the ashtray on his bed table and hands it to her, along with a pack of matches. Winny lights up, holds the smoke in her lungs for a count of ten like a pro, and then exhales through pouted lips. The pouted lips are exactly what Digby was afraid of.

"The president wants it for himself," she says.

For the life of him, Digby cannot remember what they were talking about.

"Louden's official house for its president is tiny," she goes on. "Apparently the first president was a bachelor with tidy habits. One bedroom, one bath. So this building would be perfect. But it's belonged to the Hastings family forever and they don't want to give it up."

"Not even now that Bonner is gone with no descendents?"

"Nope. Not while *Cogito* is still in business. Bonner thought the Towers had philosophical vibes. He loved this place. His great grandfather built it and three generations of Hastings were raised in it, including Bonner himself. Yankees have a thing about their family homes. They grow up getting more love out of their banisters and mantels than they do from their mothers. Do you mind if I have another toke?"

"As long as you don't intend to operate any heavy machinery," Digby says.

He should have known better. Winny immediately morphs into fleshpot mode, cupping in both hands her sizeable breasts through her Sunday frock. "Were you referring to this heavy machinery?" she simpers.

This woman teaches creative writing to Louden students? What are her kids composing—bodice-rippers? Soft-core porn? Then again, Digby's only child is not only writing erotica, but earning a fine living at it.

But what is Digby to do in this moment, which is beginning to feel eternal? His other favorite pragmatic philosopher, along with Nelson Algren, was Zorba the Greek, and Zorba insisted that it was a sin to refuse a woman who wants to make love to you. Digby, of course, is against sin.

There is a loud, frantic-sounding knock at the door. Digby prays that it is God, come to perform an intervention.

"I better get that," Digby says to Winny, leaving her with heavy machinery in hand. He opens the door to Rostislav Demidov who immediately steps inside, a look of Dostoyevskian despair on his pointy face.

"I donut eat at Norman's peas," he says. At least in Digby's present state, that is what he thinks the Russian says, so he makes a move toward the kitchenette where he hopes to find something to feed the poor fellow.

"A moment's peace," Winny says, by way of translation. "He doesn't get a moment's peace."

"Oh? What's the problem, Professor?" Digby asks.

"I am followed here and also there," he replies. It occurs to Digby that during the Cold War, while over here we were watching films about double-crossing commies, over in Leningrad they were watching films that featured sneaky Americans not giving innocent Russian citizens a moment's peace, or Norman's peas, for that matter. Cultural paranoia knows no boundaries.

"By whom?"

"Woman with binoculars."

Aha.

"That's Madeleine Follet. You know, from the magazine. She's worried about you. She thinks you're lost."

"I am nothing lost," Rosti says, sounding like a petulant dyslectic child.

"She is the maternal type. Madeleine, you know," Digby offers.

"It may be more than that," Winny pipes in, her hands, mercifully, now dangling at her sides.

"What?" Digby asks.

"I think Miss Follet has a thing for you, Professor," Winny says.

"You think a thing? That is a what?" Professor Demidov asks.

Digby has been told that Rosti Demidov, Louden's premier visiting scholar, has an international reputation in something called extensional logic, an application of logic to semantics. Digby is now quite certain that he will not steer any of his friends' children to Louden College.

"She wants to cuddle with you," Winny says. Digby admires her choice of words.

"Coddle?" Rosti asks.

"That too," Winny says.

"She has love for you," Digby adds. Actually, he rather enjoys talking in the Russian's disordered syntax; it makes him feel closer to him.

"I have no place for love," Rosti declares emphatically. It appears to be a point of pride for him. In any event, it is the clearest sentence Digby has heard him pronounce.

Rosti turns to leave and Digby panics. He has just remembered where Winny and he left off.

"Listen, Professor, I was just about to make some lunch and we'd be honored if you'd join us," he says.

"I will eat," Rostislav replies.

Divine intervention.

CHAPTER 8

Chuck Jones was once Digby's go-to smarty-pants for things African-American and ideology left of left. Although Chuck is a bona fide academic—he teaches at NYU—his prose is rhythmic, even jazzy. At *New York Magazine*, Digby often assigned him a piece about, say, break-dancers, black cross-dressers, wiretapping of cell phones, and the like. Chuck never disappointed. And so Digby is not surprised to find that the article Chuck sent him in an email attachment this fine Monday morning, a mere five days after Digby gave him the assignment, is absolutely first rate.

The title is, "St. Peter's Immigration Policy" and Digby is already smitten by the first line: "Keep them darkies outta here!" In the two thousand words that follow, good old Chuck manages to name drop Herbert Marcuse, Chris Rock, W.E.B. Dubois, William James, Snoop Dogg, St. Augustine, and Malcom X. Heaven as an elitist, racist culture. Bull's-eye! Popcult meets social philosophy spot on! Digby has tinges of yet another unexpected feeling: hopefulness.

Raised as he was by a woman who found hopefulness as Man's ultimate delusion, Digby found himself curious as to whether other metaphysicians had anything to say about it. He was not disappointed. In Bonner Hastings' personal, leather-bound library of philosophy classics stashed behind the glass-paneled doors of the bookcase to the left of his desk, Digby discovered Leibnitz's flinty optimism in his famous 'Best of All Possible Worlds' shtick. It was a tricky argument that could ultimately be summed up by a refrain Digby had frequently heard in New York City, "Could be worse"—that is, it could be worse in other possible worlds. However, a footnote in Bonner's translation of *Théodicée* led Digby straightaway to the Prince of Pessimists, Schopenhauer, whose counterargument catalogued all the evils in the universe and concluded, "If this world were a little worse, it would be no longer capable of continuing to exist. Consequently, since a worse world could not continue to exist, it is absolutely impossible; and so this world itself is the *worst of all possible worlds*." Clearly Arthur Schopenhauer was Mrs. Cynthia-Marie Maxwell's kind of guy.

Arthur and Cynthia-Marie notwithstanding, Digby does feel a buzz of optimism, so much so he even feels brave enough to open an old email in his inbox, the one from Duke University Press. Happily, it turns out to be tamer than expected, in large part because it is written in the weasel words of academia. They are "puzzled" by the theme of the new issue of *Cogito* and are "concerned about confusing readers with ambiguous structures." Ah yes, 'ambiguous structures'; Digby can relate— he is confused already. Finally, the Duke folk are withholding judgment until they see the issue to follow and will then reconsider advertising their books in the magazine. This last is the only indication that they are actually pulling their ads. *Fuck 'em.*

Next up in Digby's inbox is the spreadsheet he requested from Madeleine, the hard numbers of *Cogito* Inc. It is to laugh. Total circulation comes in at a jaw-dropping 2,100 per annum, ninety-five percent of it in subscriptions, the other five percent from newsstand sales. ("Excuse me, sir, do you have the latest issue of *Cogito* magazine? It's right there between *Christian Cowboy* and *Barely Legal*.") The subscription rate for all six annual issues is thirty bucks including postage—$7.50 a copy at the newsstand—and ad revenue amounts to $2,900 per issue. Altogether, an annual income of a little under $45,000. And that's the good news. That bad news is that it costs $25,000 more than that just to produce and mail it, and that's not counting salaries, writer fees, and overhead. But that, happily, is where the Hastings trust picks up the slack to the tune of two hundred and fifty grand a year.

Thank you, Bonner. And I have it on good authority that you can hear me up there.

Hello, what's this? A new email has appeared while Digby was reading the spreadsheet and it is from Ms. Mary Bonavitacola, subject line: "Let's talk."

Does Digby feel like doing a little dance? Nothing too gymnastic, mind you, something stately and behooving his age, like a few steps of a Morris dance. But, yes, he does indeed feel like doing a little dance.

> "Dear Digby,
> Let's talk eternity.
> Say over lunch.
> Mary"

Digby works on his reply feverishly for the next ten minutes, writing and rewriting until he feels that he strikes a fine balance between adolescent alacrity and measured maturity.

> "Dear Mary,
> I'm free today.
> Digby"

Then he sits by his Mac waiting for Mary's reply, checking the inbox every minute. When there's no reply after ten minutes, he feels an urge to assume the fetal position under his desk. He resists. At the thirty minute mark he is rewarded:

> "1 PM at Louden Clear?
> M."

Yes!

Digby arrives at the appointed spot with minutes to spare. He loiters outside the restaurant entrance assuming several casual poses, but none strike him as convincing, so he takes out a Parliament Light for a prop, letting it dangle Belmondoishly from his lower lip without lighting it. That is when, peering in Louden Clear's window, he spots his employer dining with a silver-haired man in a navy blazer. Each is leaning across the table toward the other in what looks for all the world like intimacy. Then again, the old-timers may just have hearing problems.

"Have you been waiting long?"

Digby turns to behold the Reverend Bonavitacola. She is wearing Diesel jeans and a T-shirt picturing Friedrich Nietzsche along with the philosopher's famous line, "There are no facts, only interpretations." Digby has mixed feelings. On the one hand, the Nietzsche quote strikes him as beneath her, on the other, Digby's reading of her bosom beneath Nietzsche's words is that it is considerably more voluptuous than he had remembered. He is convinced that he does not deserve to even lay his eyes upon this creature.

"Not long at all," Digby replies with some difficulty, considering the cigarette dangling from his lip. He removes and tosses it. "Listen, I see Mrs. Hastings in there. Should we find another spot?"

Mary sends Digby a quizzical look, as if he is suggesting that there is something untoward about the two of them meeting in public.

Or is it she who feels odd about their little rendezvous?

Mary surprised herself with how eagerly she went about setting up this meeting. It is not as if she is all atwitter about the prospect of writing for Cogito *magazine. Quite the opposite, in fact.*

Surely it is too early after Reuben's death for her to be even thinking about the company of another man. And, of course, that is the least of it, considering this other insane entanglement she has gotten herself into.

But the more perplexing question is, Why this flaky charac-
ter, Digby Maxwell, of all people? He is just barely attractive in
a lost puppy sort of way. And he gives off an air of New York
condescension that, in Mary's estimation, is actually New York
provincialism. Could it simply be that he is funny? It is true
that funny has been sorely missing from Mary's life for a very
long time.

"I just meant that Felicia seems deep in conversation,"
Digby says apologetically, although he is not sure what it is
he is apologizing for.

Mary peeks inside the restaurant and smiles. "Oh, yes.
Felicia's devoted lawyer. You're probably right. There's a Moroccan place over there. Do you do couscous?"

"Yes, yes."

She leads the way.

As soon as they are seated, Mary says, "How about if I
recount my story about Cape Cod and then critique Paul Tillich's essay on the eternal now? No Eckhart Tolle, promise."

"Twenty-five hundred words," Digby replies.

"Or less, I hope."

"Whatever it takes."

"I'll try my best to make it hip and *au courant*," she says.
"But I can't promise anything. I'm a little out of touch with the
zeitgeist du jour, you understand."

"So you've heard about the new mode at *Cogito?*"

"Of course, everybody has," she says. "You've been sent
to save us from our irrelevance."

Ms. Bonavitacola is obviously mocking him. Digby takes
it like a sport.

"I'm trying to thread the needle between academic philosophy and ordinary life," Digby says a tad too earnestly, then
attempts to remove the sting by adding, "You know, between
the deep and the superficial."

Miss Mary laughs.

Digby has a fleeting glimpse of paradise.

"If there's any way you can toss in something about heaven—you know, the sweet hereafter—it couldn't hurt," he says.

"I'm a Unitarian," Mary replies, grinning.

"I'll take that as a No."

After a moment, grin gone, she says, "Listen, Digby, I'm not entirely sure I'm the right person for this job. Writing—I don't know—it always makes me feel like a fraud. I don't have the gift."

Digby is at a loss for words. Or rather, several slickly witty words come to his mind, as well as several standard insincere words of comfort of the kind he often used to buck up writers like Tommy Gasparini when they had crises of confidence as deadlines approached. But none of those words seem worthy right now. So instead, he simply looks into Mary's cerulean eyes.

"Having second thoughts?" she says.

"None."

"I'm counting on you for help," she says. "Guidance."

"That's the nicest thing anybody's said to me in a long time."

"I'm serious."

"Me too."

Happily, their couscous arrives before either of them is required to speak again. They dig in.

"Last time I had couscous was in Walla Walla," Digby says after a couple of bites.

"You were with Yo Yo Ma, right?"

"No, Boutros Boutros-Ghali."

"Bishop Tutu couldn't make it?"

"No, that night he wanted seafood."

Mary closes her eyes for a minute, cogitating rapidly, then a delicious smile blossoms on her lips. She opens her eyes and cries, "Mahi-mahi! Right?"

"Absolutely!"

Their laughter rings out in the tiny Moroccan restaurant, apparently alarming their waiter who abruptly appears at their table to ask if they are still 'working' on their food. (Waiters everywhere seem to see eating as yet one more time-consuming job in people's lives.) In any event, they pay the waiter no heed. Mary has offered Digby an upturned open palm across the table and, after a moment's confusion, he slaps her five.

This initiates a whole new level of conversation, abbreviated back stories of how they each came to be here in this now. Mary married Reuben, a mathematician, while she was still in divinity school; they had no children; she had thought of becoming an academic—philosophy and theology—but then thought better of it; she loves Louden, but sometimes feels stifled here. Digby's life digest is even briefer: divorced, one child, now hoping to get to know that child better; recovering from an assortment of failures, he sees Louden as a last chance to become a functioning adult.

After lunch, Digby walks Mary back to the church. He would like to carry her books, but she doesn't have any. Mary leads, taking them on a shortcut through the college campus. Without effort, Digby is able to keep his eyes off the parade of pastel sweaters.

"After all that Swarthmore intensity, this place is a relief," Mary says.

"I haven't talked with any of the students yet. Are they as blank as they look?" Digby immediately regrets saying this. On the spot, he decides to rid himself of all New York sarcasm and snobbery. This will be Step One in his character rehabilitation to be deserving of this woman.

"I see it as openness," Mary says cheerfully.

As if on cue, a gaggle of students in jeans and matching lavender T-shirts appears from around the corner of the college library. On closer inspection, the T-shirts are not identical, being emblazoned with a variety of legends: "Gold Star Lesbian," "Gaybie," "Stromosexual," and, most intriguingly, "Hasbian." Some carry neatly lettered placards variously calling for tolerance, equality, and superior regard ("Bi's Know It ALL!").

In their midst, looking surprisingly cheery, is the gender philosopher, June MacLane, whose placard reads, "One Gender, One World." Mary waves at her and June waves back, managing to fine focus her wave so that it excludes Digby.

"Is she a friend?" Digby asks Mary.

"Yes."

"I'm afraid she doesn't like me very much," Digby says, sounding like the high school loser that he always suspected he was.

"June is very serious, very committed," Mary says.

So am I! Digby wants to snap back. But, being in spiritual rehab, he demurs. Instead, he says, "Personally, I prefer the two gender modality."

"Me too," Mary says, smiling at him. "But that's my limit. I don't go any higher than two."

Have I mentioned that I want to spend the rest of my life with Mary Bonavitacola, including bringing her breakfast in bed every morning?

In front of the church, Mary says, "When is it due?"

"Beg pardon?"

"My article."

"How about in a week?"

"Ouch!"

"Okay, ten days. It's my last offer."

"But what if I just can't do it?"

"You can."

"But what if I can't?"

"I'll think of a suitable penance."

Mary laughs and offers Digby a hand to shake. He would like to leverage that proffered hand into a pull into his arms, but once again he resists his dual-gender impulses. They shake hands like business partners.

"Meantime, I may call you for guidance," Mary says as she turns toward the church door.

Digby waits until she is inside to finally execute his Morris dance.

CHAPTER 9

According to the popular songs of Digby's father's youth—the songs his father had listened to every Sunday evening via Time-Life's *Magic of Love* boxed, 33⅓ RPM set—people in love invariably experience an altered worldview. Gone are *Weltschmerz*, petty thoughts, and weather worries. In are ambient optimism, generosity of spirit, and the perception that everyone else is either also in love or on the brink of it. A lyric example: "When the stars make you drool just like a pasta fazool, that's amore."

So it is that when Digby returns to his office and sees Rostislav Demidov and Madeleine Follet whispering to one another at her desk, he finds himself mentally drooling, pasta fazoolishly. Love conquers all, apparently including unintelligible communication. As Digby approaches, he sees a new, snappy looking GPS sitting on top of Madeleine's desk. Wrapping paper and a red ribbon lie beside it. A gift borne of love.

"You make me an insult," Rosti is intoning.

Perhaps, Digby decides, he has altered his worldview too soon.

"It's just so you always know where you are, Rosti," Madeleine replies tenderly. She, at least, remains in the pasta fazool zone.

"I know I am where," Rosti counters. "Here!"

Digby realizes that he has not asked Professor Demidov if he would like to contribute to the Heaven Issue of *Cogito*.

Perhaps he could create an extensional logic acrostic that spells out Shangri-la.

Madeleine looks up at Digby. "A woman called."

Mary?

"Who? Should I call back?" Digby replies excitedly. He feels no need to hide his fervor around a fellow/sister lovestruckee.

"She didn't leave her name. She'll call back."

Aha, so, Mary and he are already at the secret communication stage.

"And don't forget the president's cocktail party this afternoon," Madeleine continues.

"The president?"

"President Herker. In the faculty common room."

"Are you sure I'm invited?"

"Everybody is. Oh, and we got two more cancellations. Indiana U and Oxford. Pulled their book ads."

"For a grand total of how much?"

"I don't know. Something like twelve hundred."

"Dollars? Oh my goodness." Although Digby is committed to a thorough character makeover, he is not quite ready to abandon all sarcasm. He fears that would leave huge gaps of dead air in his day-to-day interactions.

"This came in a little while ago. Postage due."

She hands Digby a plain brown envelope with the words PLAIN BROWN ENVELOPE stamped on it—an old Tommy Gasparini prank.

In his office, Digby opens the envelope with the antique bronze letter knife that came with Bonner Hastings' oak desk. Inside are seven illustrated pages from Tommy, starting with a Hogarth woodblock print of St. Jerome gazing at heaven and ending with a Kacho Oji animé from a series called *The Legend of Lost Heaven*. Digby's read-through of the accompanying text confirms his first impression: the piece is brilliant, visually dazzling, insightful, and a hoot.

Digby removes his shoes, leans back in his swivel chair, lifts his stockinged feet onto his desk, and gazes out through the window at the budding wildflowers and beyond, the quad of Louden College. By God, he feels good. First Chuck and now Tommy have come through for him with first class articles, applying Manhattan smarts to old school subject matter. Classic wit meets the classics. Not only is the renovated *Cogito* going to be a true original, but maybe Digby truly is the man for the job. The ad pulls by those stodgy university presses are actually a testimony to his innovative genius; they simply cannot keep up with him. In fact, in this precious moment, Digby feels he is finally fulfilling his early promise in a way he never imagined. He feels absolved of all irony, so much so that the roach his fingers encounter in his jacket pocket seems an adolescent relic. And then, of course, there is Mary. A woman of both wit and substance. What an absurd and wondrous combination. Is she to be included in his newborn destiny?

The phone rings. From down the hall, Madeleine yells, "That woman again."

Digby removes his feet from the desk in an act of decorum. It is the least he can do for Mary.

"Hello?"

"I need your mailing address." A woman's voice, not Mary's. Digby cannot immediately identify whose voice it is, but it is just familiar enough to send a *shpritz* of gastric acid up to the back of his throat.

"Is this—?"

"Yes. Sylvia's mother."

That would be Digby's former wife. "How are you, Fanny?"

"You are behind in Sylvia's tuition," Fanny says.

"That's because she's no longer in school."

"That's irrelevant."

For a junior partner at a tony Manhattan law firm, Fanny's grasp of fundamental logic—for example, Aristotle's Law of the Excluded Middle ('A' is either true or it is not true, it cannot be anything in between)—is subpar. Then again, maybe the relationship between legal thinking and logical thinking is weak at best. Nonetheless, with this argument, Fanny has reached a new low in garbage reasoning, right up there with the Tea Party activists. Digby has always found it more difficult to argue with blatant illogic than with coherent stupidity: it is harder to know where to begin.

"She's supporting herself, Fanny. She told me so herself."

"That tuition money is part of my general expenses," Fanny says. Digby thinks he understands what she is saying this time: Fanny has been pocketing his tuition payments, and further, she is quite certain that she is morally entitled to do so.

Although Digby readily admits that he treated Fanny badly in his late shithead period, he is not quite ready to let her establish the penalty for his transgressions, especially with the benefit of sophistic moral reasoning. In any event, punishment certainly appears to be what Fanny must be after, not subsistence. At this point, she earns roughly four times what Digby does.

"This sounds like a problem for the lawyers," Digby says.

"Exactly. What's your mailing address?"

Digby gives it, then adds, "Not that you're interested, but things are going well up here."

Predictably, Fanny responds by hanging up. Digby smiles. He is proud of himself. This is one Fanny guilt trip that never lifted anchor. Digby even detects a charitable wish in his heart, fleeting as it is: he hopes that Fanny can get on with her life as happily as she is able. Yes, he actually feels that. His character improvement program is working absolutely splendidly.

By the time he finishes doing a quick first edit of Tommy's article (Tommy always had a proclivity for run-on sentences, some running the length of the page, and this piece is no exception), it is time for Digby to suit up for the president's late afternoon cocktail party. The occasion, Madeleine informed him, is Herker's annual Rite of Spring and its purpose is to build faculty camaraderie before the end of the spring term, by which time it would then be too late to build anything.

Despite the fact that Digby's array of ties is down to three— a black clip-on bow for weddings and funerals, an Italian paisley that looks like a high-end Rorschach Test, and his threadbare Christmas tie sprinkled with portraits of Santa and his helpers—he spends a good five minutes dithering over his choice. Usually, he dons the paisley number only when he is feeling particularly insecure and out-of-place, so it seems the natural choice for today's outing; but when he considers the possibility that Mary might be there, he has second thoughts—she might find it tacky. Still, he tries it on and looks in the mirror. He decides it makes him look overripe, a floral arrangement going to seed at the top—his face. So the black clip-on bow it is, and Digby is pleased with the overall effect—the can't-be-bothered-tying-his-own-tie nerd-genius.

There is a spring in his step as he saunters down Brigham Street to the Rite of Spring fete. He catches a glimpse of his bow-tied self reflected in Write Now's window; he decides he looks rakish and vaguely mysterious. A stranger in town. *Who is he? What does he want? Will Louden ever be the same after he has trod its streets?* As he nears the quad, he hears ethereal voices rising up, obviously the mystery man's theme music. Not exactly, for he now sees that the strains issue from a lavender-shirted chorus gathered under a budding willow on the sward. It is the gay cohort singing "Crucified."

The party is in full swing when Digby arrives, a good thirty or forty folk chattering and laughing. The reception room on the ground floor of the Administration Building is ablaze with flowers, the gold-framed oil portraits of Louden's past presidents draped with plastic ivy (these men appear considerably more optimistic than the Harvard past presidents hung on the Harvard Club's walls), and here and there, white linen-covered card tables bearing drinks and nuts manned by students in white shirts and—*oops*—black clip-on bow ties. The mystery man is done for. Digby quickly removes and pockets his tie; he is content to be taken for a nerd, but he draws the line at being taken for the help.

"Martini, sir?" one of the help asks.

"Uh, yes. But hold the vermouth."

A few feet away, a tall baby-faced man with a full crop of khaki-colored hair, is waving enthusiastically at Digby. Digby knows who it is: President Miles "Kim" Herker, himself. It would be impossible not to recognize him; the man's image is virtually everywhere in Louden: on the cover of every college publication, including the hand-out map of the campus; virtually every week on the front page of the local weekly; and—Mao-like—on posters affixed to walls and trees announcing meetings, lectures, and even sports events. Along with his face, Herker's reputation—especially among faculty members—precedes him. To put it delicately, he is better known for his ability to raise money from alums than for his ability to think in anything resembling a linear modality, not that Digby was ever naïve enough to believe that these two aptitudes were in any way related.

Digby walks up to him and offers his hand. "I'm Digby Maxwell, the new editor—"

Herker grabs Digby's hand and yanks him toward his going-to-flab, former-football-player chest. "Hell, I know who you are, Mr. Maxwell. Everybody does. You're our new celebrity."

He gives Digby a couple of good raps on the back before releasing him and Digby is relieved, having feared there was going to be some of that new, manly cheek kissing.

"Hardly a celebrity," Digby demurs, working up an 'aw-shucks' expression on his brow.

"Maybe not in big bad New York," Herker laughs. "But up here in Louden, you're the max."

"That's certainly something I've always wanted to be," Digby replies, doing a little boyish chortling himself.

"What's that?"

"The max," Digby says. He gets the feeling this conversation is not going well so he segues with, "Speaking of which, early spring up here is lovely."

"You said it, Maxwell," President Herker says, placing a fleshy hand on his shoulder. "Springtime in Louden is enough to make an old man's sap run."

Clearly, Digby's resolve to rid himself of all Manhattan snobbery is being tested. Sorely. He decides that his best option is to move on as quickly as possible, and he sees an opportunity to excuse himself gracefully in the form of a diminutive, tightly-corseted redhead with sumptuous lips who has sauntered up to Herker.

"Well, I don't want to monopolize you, Mr. Herker," Digby says, nodding toward the redhead and feinting to Herker's left. Digby is pleased that his grasp of cocktail party choreography is still intact.

"Please call me Kim. And don't be running away now—I want you to get to know my little Muffy."

"Your muffy, sir?"

Herker swings a meaty arm around the pinched waist of the redhead. "Muffy's one of your biggest fans," he says.

"I am a New Yorker *moi-même*," Muffy says, winking at Digby. "I slip back down to the Big Apple whenever my lord and master isn't looking."

Digby shakes little Muffy's hand; it is moist and limp. She is searching his face, looking, he believes, for traces of exoticism, perhaps a sign that he is the real thing—a New York Jew.

"That's a long *schlep*," Digby says obligingly. Lenny Bruce once quipped, "If you live in New York and you're Catholic, you're still Jewish."

"I am so glad to finally meet you, Mr. Maxwell," Muffy says. "I have a little favor I've been dying to ask you and now I finally can."

"No harm in asking," Digby replies.

"We have a little group that meets on Thursday mornings. We call it the Thursday Morning Club. And we would be enchanté if you would be our guest next week. Our *invité d'honneur*."

"Sure, I guess so. What would be expected of me?"

Muffy issues a vaguely coquettish smile. "Oh, just be yourself," she says.

"That can be chancy," Digby replies. "I have multiple personality disorder."

This occasions a veritable howl of mirth from the first lady of Louden College. Her husband, who appears to have had the same amount of difficulty following their little *tête-à-tête* as Digby has, starts chortling too. Digby's guess is that Kim Herker has generally found it expedient to follow his wife's lead; among other virtues, it makes him appear more quick-witted.

"All this wonderful laughter! I should have guessed you'd be at the center of it, Digby." This from Felicia Hastings who has sidled up beside Digby, her silver-haired lawyer a discrete two steps behind her.

Felicia merits a double bear hug from Herker but, Digby observes, only a coolish handshake from his missus, while the Silver Fox merely garners a polite nod from each. From somewhere beyond the Administration Building patio come the strains of "I Am What I Am" in quaint, close harmonies more in keeping with 'N Sync than Gloria Gaynor. Undoubtedly the gay choir.

"How lovely," Felicia says. "I heard we were going to have some light entertainment."

Herker gives a shrug that says, in effect, 'Nothing I could do about it' and Digby takes this opportunity to finally slip away, but not before Muffy does an elaborate pantomime in his direction, a dumb show of a phone call—to be from her to him, he presumes.

After a few steps, Digby gazes around, considering his options. Straight ahead he sees Elliot Goldenfield, sporting a seersucker suit and, of all things, white buck shoes. Digby is now convinced that Elliot has an identity problem even more confused than his own. To his right, Digby sees Winny in a diaphanous peasanty number holding court at the center of a group of male junior faculty members. Digby is pleased by her popularity; he also feels relieved by it. He skirts around her group observing that he has only been in town a few weeks and he already has a roster of people to be skirted. Actually, this realization makes him feel at home. On his left, he hears a new serenade, a rendition of Queen's "I'm in Love with My Car." Digby turns to face the music and that is when the floor-to-ceiling window in front of him shatters.

He jumps back just in time to dodge the projectile that did the shattering—a Coors beer bottle—and a light rain of glass shards. A hush followed by screams. Kim Herker charges up beside Digby. For a second, Digby suspects that Herker believes he broke the window himself, and the fact that Digby is pointing at the beer bottle at his feet only supports Herker's hunch. But now, beyond the jaggedly open window, they see a swarm of young people. Two swarms, actually. One is the lavender T-shirted serenaders, the other a more motley group T-shirt-wise—some of these varsity team T-shirts, others, "Young Republicans" T-shirts, still others, "Tea Party Republicans" T-shirts, and then the cutest of the lot, "Beer Party Republicans" T-shirts picturing Uncle Sam quaffing down a can of Bud Lite. This non-gay swarm appears to have a big tent policy, including in their number blazer-clad preppies, jocks, some gangly, Louden day students, and a few earnest Christians of the sort that Jeremiah Louden would have surely approved, two of them actually holding Bibles at their sides. A good number of this more loosely associated pack have glazed, beer-besotted eyes as a common denominator.

Digby trusts that President Herker has little doubt which group is responsible for the broken window. Both groups are frozen in their tracks. It is at this moment that Digby spots Reverend Mary out there, standing beside June MacLane. Digby notes that Mary is wearing one of those lavender T-shirts herself, hers emblazoned with the legend, "Do you know WHAT your child is?" Digby consoles himself by recalling her stated allegiance to the two-gender modality.

The Rite of Spring guests have gathered just behind Herker and Digby, most still clinging to their martini glasses. With amazing grace, Herker stoops down and worms his hulk through the broken window onto the lawn. For reasons that Digby cannot begin to fathom, he worms through after Herker.

"Whoever did this, step forward," Herker says in a surprisingly temperate yet authoritative tone. Digby immediately takes back every patronizing thought he had about Herker; this man is a leader of men, something Digby believes he would have been if he had managed to become a totally different person.

No one, however, steps forward, although there is a lot of shifty-eyed eye shifting in the bleary-eyed Beer Party Republican contingent. A few of them now issue some nasal snickering, culminating in an anonymous yelp of, "Musta been one of the fudge packers!" This witticism elicits a few baritone guffaws. And that is when Digby spots another beer bottle aloft.

As if in TV instant replay, Digby watches the bottle sail through the air in slow motion, reach its peak, and arc downward. It is headed directly for the ash-blonde crown of his beloved Mary.

It should be noted here that, much to his father's disappointment, Digby is absent athletic inclination and ability. To please his father, Digby once volunteered to be the placekick holder on the Passaic High football team, but he was dismissed after the third time he reflexively withdrew his finger before the kicker's foot met the ball.

But love, as they say, is a drug, and in Digby's case it is apparently adrenaline. He charges forward and leaps, Kobe-like, toppling a pair of gold star lesbians in his path and—right arm stretched high—snatches the bottle in midair. He returns to his feet at Mary's side.

The cheer that goes up both inside the party room and out on the lawn is more than enough to make Digby wish he had followed his father's ambitions for him. He half expects to be gathered up and hoisted atop shoulders to be paraded around the campus. Reverend Mary Bonavitacola reaches up her face to Digby's and kisses his cheek.

"Nice catch," she says.

"It was nothing," Digby says, channeling the high school gridiron hero he once longed to be.

Herker then approaches Digby and gives him a muscular hug more taxing on his heart-lung package than the bottle-snag itself. In mid-hug, Herker whispers somewhat forbiddingly into Digby's ear, "Show off!" and then gives him what used to be called in Passaic High School a noogie. Digby endures it, puzzled.

Then, abruptly, it is all over. Digby's athletic leap had denouement written all over it. Both groups of students immediately disperse, Mary vanishing with them. 'Whoever did this' has not stepped forward, but nonetheless Herker, looking triumphant, clambers back inside where the floor is already being swept clean of glass. And Digby is left alone, intercepted beer bottle in hand. A stranger in town.

CHAPTER **10**

Wen it comes to the question of Digby's attractiveness to women, the man in question has few delusions. Digby readily acknowledges that he is not a particularly sexy fellow, never has been. He appears to have been born resolutely heterosexual and possesses a normal appetite as such, but he cannot say that women were ever especially drawn to him upon first look. He has a face that vanishes all too easily in a crowd, perhaps one reason why assuming other people's identities comes so easily to him: doggie-brownish hair and eyes, a narrow nose that has always drifted slightly eastward, and a mouth that tends to droop open like a carp on the prowl. Neither ugly nor handsome but, if there is any plus on the visual side, decidedly male. Nay, it has been his sporadic wit and occasional well-timed gag that has lured his fair share of women into bed with him, all of them far more attractive than he. This is patently unfair, he knows: a woman as plain as he is cannot as successfully compensate in the sexual marketplace with a good joke as he can. But Digby takes no responsibility for that inequality; he did not legislate the laws of attraction.

In any event, this helps explain his reluctance to work on that part of himself that habitually takes nothing seriously: that part is the mother of his wit. And his wit got him bedmates.

Dr. Epstein, who a few generations back would have been a far better rabbi than he is now a psychiatrist, found Digby's dilemma existential in its proportions. He believed Digby needed to give his basic, serious self a chance to reemerge and to this end he put him in group therapy—Epstein's theory being that once Digby saw his superficial self on display in front of a sensitive audience, he would see the wisdom in dropping his wiseass façade.

It was not to be so. In fact, from Epstein's point of view, it worked out ass backwards, in a manner of speaking. On the other hand, it did change the course of Digby's life.

At the time of his first group session, Digby was on his third job, employed as a copy editor at *Food Stylist* magazine, correcting the grammar and remodeling the syntax of writers who saw a porcelain plate as a canvas on which to aesthetically balance the daring swoop of a charred wisp of shallot with the blatant thereness of a broiled sea scallop. The utter absurdity of the whole enterprise worked to Digby's advantage—it was inherently beyond the scope of his irony. That and the fact that he was sequestered in a freestanding, opaque glass cubicle kept him from peppering his coworkers with his reflexive wiseass-isms. Epstein saw the job as a step in the right direction; Digby saw it as a step to oblivion.

Digby's first thought on taking his place at the circle of bridge chairs and glancing at his co-therapees was that he wished he had worn a snappier-looking shirt. Upon virtually every other chair was perched a good-looking woman, albeit a sad-eyed and joyless one.

"Have I come to the right room?" he said deadpan. "I'm looking for the Welcome Wagon Pep Squad."

Laughter. Oodles of it.

Epstein then got the session rolling by asking Karen—she of golden ringlets and dolorous grey eyes—how her week had gone. Not well at all, as it turned out. She had endured a two-hour conversation with her mother in New Haven on the subject of body stockings. Digby is now a little hazy on the details, but the New Haven mom saw them as a sign of the era's moral decay. Epstein asked Karen what she thought the conversation was really about, but the poor girl drew a blank, so Epstein threw it open for general discussion.

The young woman next to Digby ventured, "It sounds like your mother thinks body stockings are provocative. You know, like you are just inviting men to hit on you. She just doesn't know, you know?"

A sparkling analysis, Epstein said. Anyone else?

The handsomest man in the room, a chiseled-featured fellow in his early thirties, offered, "I'm thinking of scary stuff. Like a stocking over your face like in the *Boogeyman*."

Epstein asked him to develop his idea further, but Handsome responded rather gruffishly that he thought his film allusion spoke for itself.

Anyone else?

"You know, Karen, I'm trying to see this from your mother's point of view, so I need to get an idea of what she herself would look like in a body stocking," Digby said earnestly.

Epstein eyed him warily, but Karen, the poor sweetie, smiled. "Not so good," she murmured. "Her thighs, you know?"

"So in a body stocking she'd look like hog shanks in pajamas," Digby said with just the hint of a twinkle in his doggie-brownish eyes.

No one would need to advise Digby that his quip was wit-free. It was sixth grade repartee. It doesn't even make much sense. Digby knew that then and he knows it now. But he also knew from long experience that the word 'pajamas' is funny; it simply has a funny sound that makes people laugh, which is exactly what it did in that group therapy session. Raucous, bent-over-at-the-waist laughter.

In that instant Digby made two luminous observations. First, this group of sad sacks was the easiest audience he had ever encountered. So woe were they that any opportunity to express a little mirth was manna from heaven. A clown hat would have been enough to do the trick. It actually helped that they were impounded there for the sole purpose of doing some serious work on their sorrowful innards; that somehow excused and legitimatized a little merriment.

Digby's second observation was that his sex life was about to take a dramatic upturn.

It most certainly did, including amorous encounters with roughly half of the women in the group. (It should be noted that Digby's material improved considerably as the weeks went by.) But that in itself certainly does not qualify as life-changing in any long term sense. What does was Digby's stunning insight a few months later that group therapy was the best damned pickup bar in New York City.

For the first time in his adult life, Digby took one of his Manhattan cultural insights seriously and so proceeded to write an article about this therapy-*qua*-pickup-bar phenomenon—wrote it at a single sitting, no less. Shamelessly, he even quoted his "hog shanks in pajamas" line as an example of how low the threshold of wit could be and still allow the therapee to get lucky. Then Digby mailed the article off to *The Village Voice* where they accepted it in two days' time and then published it on page three under the headline, "Group Sex." It got mail, lots of it.

Phil Winston phoned Digby soon thereafter. He wanted to know if Digby had any other ideas for articles for the *Voice*. Digby rattled half a dozen off the top of his head, most of them involving the sexual habits of his age group, but also including such topics as how basketball slang creeps into Wall Street jargon, why the belt, as we know it, is heading for obsolescence, and how illegal aliens from Chile have cornered the sushi *sous chef* market. Two days later, Phil offered Digby a staff job. He took it. And thus did his estimable career as a wiseass prophet begin and flourish.

For obvious reasons, the publication of his article also marked the conclusion of his therapy, both private and group.

CHAPTER **11**

For the past three weeks, Digby has been serene bordering on beatific. Mary and he have lunched twice again on Moroccan fare, jabbering and laughing while purportedly going over drafts of her article about the Eternal Now. No, they have not smooched; in truth, they have barely touched except for lingering handshakes at the church door. But this, too, is at one with Digby's heartsease. He feels they are courting and he feels courtly, a man of grace and deep feeling. He remains sanguine that he is remaking himself into someone worthy of her.

Paradoxically, Digby's new chasteness has turned him into a more tolerant—even enthusiastic—reader and occasional editor of Sylvia's online serial baud-fest, *The Unmade Bed*. He reads it daily now, often with genuine twinges of parental pride, admiring such phrases as "His body had a musty odor, somewhere between the perfume of an overused bath towel and refried beans." And, "It was not so much a climax as a presumed outcome." *My little girl!* He often emails her his compliments, occasionally along with an idea for an editorial tweak, and she writes back, "Thnx" or sometimes even, "Thnx D." Digby likes to think that "D" stands for Dad.

To top things off, putting together his first issue of *Cogito* is feeling more and more like a personal mission, one for which not only Felicia Hastings had chosen him, but the Fates themselves. So it is this morning as he enters Hastings Towers after his now-routine morning ramble to and from Uncommon Grounds where he downs three cups of locally roasted coffee along with a marmalade scone, that there is a bounce of exuberance in his step. He is still bouncing when he enters his office and sees Madeleine Follet perched on the Victorian settee across from his desk.

"Good morning, good morning, it's a beautiful day." Digby surprises himself by unconsciously mimicking the cheery tones of Mr. Rogers, whose kiddy show reruns he had watched religiously during his stoned sojourn on Bleecker Street.

"Now he's lost his GPS," Madeleine says.

"Is there a GPS finder?" Digby asks jauntily, but he sees immediately that he is not taking this crisis seriously enough, so he goes on, "Actually, maybe it would be a good idea to attach one of those finder things to Rosti. You know, like you put on your reading glasses or your dog."

"He'd lose that too."

"Isn't there something he always has on him? A watch? His passport?"

"Well, there is his notebook. He never goes anywhere without it."

"Bingo!" Digby says, and Madeleine rises, full of purpose.

Digby smiles. Whatever his faults may still be, he has always prided himself on being helpful.

"Oh, somebody called this morning," Madeleine says in parting. "Somebody named Binx Berger. I left his number on your desk."

Binx Berger? Head writer for Saturday Night Live*? How many Binx Bergers could there be?*

Digby remains standing as he dials the number.

"Binx here."

"Digby Maxwell returning your call."

"Hi guy." *Guy?* Digby has never met this guy, just spied him once or twice at cocktail and book parties in his heyday.

"Listen, there's some buzz going around about your magazine," says Binx.

Buzz? About Cogito? *In the Big Apple?*

Digby becomes giddy; giddiness becomes him.

"Down there in my old hometown, eh?" Digby says as casually as his outbreak of delirium permits.

"In the Waverly Inn to be exact. Ran into Tommy Gasparini at one end of the bar, Chuck Jones at the other."

Digby suddenly remembers how small a town New York actually is: two different people whispering about the same thing in the same tony bar can create a gale wind of scuttlebutt. The word 'edgy' is uttered, then the phrase 'outside the box,' then, *sotte voce*, the topper of all toppers, 'this is definitely the very next thing.' Come to think of it, it was in just such a way that Digby used to detect subject matter for *New York Magazine*.

"How can I help you, Binx?" Digby says.

"I'd like to take a crack at a piece about heaven."

"For *Cogito*, right?"

"*Gesundheit.*"

Digby laughs politely. Then, "Funny stuff?"

"No, deep. Deeply funny."

"Sounds promising. Any ideas?"

"Just a title. But it says it all."

Binx pauses, so Digby says, "I'm all ears, Binx."

" 'Your Afterlife Has Been Pre-Recorded.' "

Digby has no idea what Binx Berger has in mind with this title, but this is of little import because all Digby can see is his byline, 'Binx Berger, Head Writer, *Saturday Night Live*.' In the old days at *New York Magazine*, the likes of Binx never even responded to Digby when he floated an article idea in their direction.

Yes, I am the Phoenix, rising from the ashes of failure. My life does *have a second act!*

"Wow, Binx! That's fabulous."

"Say, fifteen hundred words?"

"Perfect."

"By when?"

"Two weeks?"

"Done."

"Binx, I should tell you that I'm working on a restricted budget here."

He laughs. "You mean I'm not going to get rich off your philosophy magazine?"

"Not in this life," Digby says.

Binx offers the indulgent snicker of a highly paid funnyman and they bid their farewells. Still standing, Digby experiences a rush of empowerment over his coup and, as is his wont, immediately casts about for someone to whom to display his surge of self-confidence before it dissipates. So he decides to personally deliver the news of the Binx Berger plum to his resident backbiters, June MacLane and Elliot Goldenfield. Actually, he has not exchanged a word with either of them in weeks; it has been like sharing an apartment with an ex-wife during a housing shortage.

As Digby prepares to knock on their office door, he hears June's voice rising; she apparently is in the midst of a testy telephone conversation. Digby does what any man who is deeply interested in the lives of other people would do: he lowers his hand and eavesdrops.

"I don't give a shit what he thinks," Ms. MacLane is saying. "I'm just not daddy's little girl anymore. I'm my own person."

Pause.

"He can't do that! He gave that stock to me! I have the certificate."

Pause.

"That's legal mumbo-jumbo. I'm still me. I am who I am and I own what I own."

Pause, during which Digby finds himself admiring June's locution for combining biblical cadences with capitalist ideology.

"Mom, please. We need the money. Listen, I wasn't going to tell you this way, but we're having a baby. That's why we need that money."

With this last, June's voice has not only changed tone but register, creeping up to the pitch of somebody's little girl. Another pause and then, "No, *I'm* pregnant. But it's *her* egg."

Digby suddenly senses a presence behind him. He turns to see Elliot Goldenfield's glare.

"Oh, am I in your way?" Digby asks ingenuously.

"You have no shame at all, do you, Maxwell?" Goldenfield simpers. "Apparently you haven't read Hobbes on the sanctity of privacy."

"Afraid I'm stuck in my natural state," Digby replies, pretty sure there is a philosophy joke buried in there somewhere.

Goldenfield pushes by Digby, opens the door, slips in, and slams the door in front of him.

Digby's sense of empowerment feels flimsy.

Chapter 12

Unbidden, a fully illuminated memory comes: Digby is lying spread-eagle on his back on the banks of Yantacaw Pond in Passaic. In his mouth is the Hohner Blues Harp harmonica he has recently received for his eleventh birthday. With an unfocused gaze, he is staring at the cloudless sky. He breathes through his mouth through the harmonica, evoking a simple triad followed by the same triad a half tone lower. In, out; major, minor.

Then, from out of the blue, his mind jumps out of his head. He sees himself lying there. He hears his simple chords. He has an astounding thought—the sound he is producing by simply breathing is part of All Sound, part of the Sound of the Universe. This effortless epiphany fills him with sublime joy. He is at one with Oneness. It is his Buddha moment. And then, of course, it is gone in a minute and he is just a boy dawdling on his way home from school and he had better get moving or Mom will be mad.

In real time, Digby is sitting at his kitchen table in his apartment in Hastings Towers. The vivid Blues Harp memory, submerged for three decades, tingles both mind and body. He had been reading theologian Paul Tillich's essay "The Eternal Now" in a collection of essays titled *The Meaning of Death*, and had become mesmerized by these lines: "There is no other way of judging time than to see it in the light of the eternal. In order to judge something, one must be partly within it, partly out of it." That is when this boyhood moment came flying back to him.

The essay was part of his homework for his upcoming meeting with Mary, but this cannot wait. He dials her number.

Only after her phone has rung several times does he check his watch: it is almost midnight. He decides to hang up, but then Mary answers with a sleepy, "Hello?"

Digby's first impulse is to hit the End-Call button on his phone so he can escape without embarrassment, but the sound of her voice trumps that urge.

"It's Digby. I'm sorry, Mary. I lost track of the time. We'll talk tomorrow."

"Hey, I had to get up to answer the phone anyhow," Mary says. It's an old gag and Digby loves it.

"I only wanted to tell you that I think I finally get that Eternal Now thing. Or at least something like it."

"Are you serious?" She is clearly fully awake now.

"Yup. But I've got to warn you, it's pretty banal."

"Those are my favorite kind."

Digby tells Mary his Sound of the Universe memory. She says nothing.

"Did I put you back to sleep?" he asks.

"No. Just the opposite. Do you want to have a drink? Louden Clear is still open."

Mary is already standing outside the bar when Digby arrives. She wears a well-tailored trench coat over what are obviously pajamas. The Unitarians are a casual sect. They greet each other and head inside. They both order brandies before they speak to one another again.

"I love your harmonica story," she says, finally.

"It was buried pretty deep. Didn't have a clue it was in there. I was reading Tillich when it popped up."

"Only the very best theology can do that," Mary says. She laughs and Digby joins in just for the sheer pleasure of laughing with her.

"But here's the puzzle," he says. "That insight—or whatever—came and went, you know? No traces left behind. It's probably the only transcendental moment I've ever had and I was eleven years old at that. And I've been slogging along in the everyday world ever since."

Mary says nothing, simply gazes with her brilliant blue eyes into Digby's. It takes him a moment before he sees the tears collecting in the inner corners of these wondrous eyes. She wipes them with the sleeve of her coat, then says, "Me too. Ain't that the shits?"

"Yup."

"If we were really brave or committed or something, we'd just cut out for a Bodhi tree somewhere and sit under it until we heard the cosmic music again," Mary says.

"Who's got the time?" Digby says and they both smile.

"At least with forty days and forty nights on the desert, you have some parameters. You know, you could save up vacation time for that," she says.

They laugh, raise their snifters, and clink.

"To the blessed moments," Mary says.

"All one of them," Digby replies.

Finally, Digby asks the question that had been troubling him in his late-in-life, late-at-night philosophy studies.

"This stuff you've got me reading is awfully hard, Mary. Tillich, Kierkegaard, Buber. Really and truly, I can't begin to grasp most of it and I used to be a fairly decent student. So what about other people, people who just don't get the hang of abstract thinking? Do they get left out in the cold?"

"You mean, is it just another brand of elitism?"

"Well, now that you mention it."

Mary closes her eyes and shakes her fine-featured face back and forth a couple of times before responding. "You, Mr. Maxwell, have just asked the sixty-four thousand dollar question. The one that finally made up my mind about going to graduate school. *Not* going, that is. If there is one thing in the world that should not be reserved for the select few, it's the philosophical underpinnings of faith, for God's sake."

"Amen," Digby says and Mary laughs. She reaches across the table and takes his hand in hers, squeezes it, and then, embarrassed, lets it go.

"You know, I'm starting to think that Bonner Hastings was on to something with the magazine," she says. "Make this stuff available to everybody. Even make it funny. Why not, for God's sake? To tell you the truth, Digby, I've been racking my brain day and night about how to make my article funny. But I simply don't have the gift."

"Funny isn't everything," he says. He means it for a change.

Mary responds by digging around in the side pockets of her trench coat. She withdraws a folded piece of paper, unfolds it, and sets it on the table in front of her.

"I've been carrying this around everywhere I go for a few days," she says, her expression somewhere between sheepish and giddy. She nervously presses out the creases in the paper before she goes on, "I can't be funny myself, but I do know funny when I see it. Anyway, just for fun, you know, I started keeping a list of clever things people have said about heaven."

Digby smiles and nods encouragingly.

"This one's from Tom Stoppard," Mary says. "'Eternity's a terrible thought. I mean, when's it all going to end?'"

They both giggle.

"Next?" Digby says.

"Okay, this one's from Mark Twain. 'When I think about the number of disagreeable people that I know who have gone to a better world, I am sure hell won't be so bad at all.'"

More giggles.

"Okay, here's my absolute favorite. Woody Allen. 'I do not believe in an afterlife, although just in case I am bringing a change of underwear.'"

With this one, their giggling gets out of hand, edging ever so closely to hysteria.

Indeed, it is not simply the Woody Allen line that sends their laughter in the direction of hysteria. For both of them, if for different reasons, it is the raucous laughter of long-suppressed and just-released anxiety, their existential corks popping.

Around them, other Louden Clear customers go quiet and gaze at them, most of them smiling. Only now does Digby take in the other late-night denizens of the college hangout, mostly students in groups of two or three gulping down beer, many of them with open books on the tables in front of them. In the far corner, near the kitchen door, he spots his original Louden Clear mates, Winny and her glum professor cadre. Of this group, only Winny smiles. She offers Digby a little trill of her fingers. He nods back, looking a little more shamefaced than intended and she looks away.

"Unfinished business?" Mary says. Their laughter vacation is over.

"Nope, finished. That may be the problem."

"I'm sorry. None of my business. Louden's a small town, in case you hadn't noticed."

"I'd noticed. No problem."

A few minutes later, they are silently walking the Louden campus. The willows are now leafy enough to rustle as they mosey by. From an open dorm window, they hear Miles Davis's "Flamenco Sketches" from his masterful *Kind of Blue* sessions. There's hope for these Louden kids yet. Mary takes Digby's hand.

I am eleven years old! The second time today! Actually, it seems like a good age to start my life over again, especially with its pre-puberty clarity.

Digby squeezes her hand. Mary lets go.

"I'm not going to sleep with you," she says.

Digby's heart momentarily ceases functioning. "Ever?"

"Probably not."

Funny, be funny, goddamn it! "Was it something I said?"

"It's not a joke, I'm afraid."

"I don't need to rush things, if that's what's worrying you."

"There's more to it than that," Mary says. "A whole lot more."

Their gait has slowed to half time, but neither of them has the strength or the bravery to look at one another. There are obvious questions: Is she still in mourning for Reuben? Has she taken a vow of some sort? Is she involved with someone else? Is Digby still more of an obvious shithead than he thinks he is or wants to be? But before he can select which question comes first, Mary says, "I'm afraid I've gotten myself into one hell of a pickle."

"Does this pickle have a name?"

"I can't say. Not now. Probably not ever. I'm sorry. I think I'll go on alone now, okay? Good night, Digby. This has been the loveliest evening."

Her words are swallowed up in the Silence of the Universe.

CHAPTER 13

"This is crazy!" is Digby's greeting from Madeleine as he returns from his morning coffee ramble. Digby keeps moving. He is far too preoccupied with Mary's inscrutable pickle to wish to hear the latest move in Madeleine's game of hide-and-seek with the sour Russian.

"They want the entire back page and both inside cover pages. I didn't even know what price to give them," Madeleine says.

"Who does?"

"Saatchi."

"Who?" Digby stops in his tracks.

"I don't know. It's an advertising agency. Or at least that's what they said they were."

"Saatchi & Saatchi?"

"That's what I said."

Digby circles back and sits down across from Madeleine. She pushes a sheet of paper across her desk to him. On it are her phone notes: "Clive Bosnoglian. Account executive. Sachy x 2. NYC. 3 full-page ads (bk + inside covers). Cost? RSVP ASAP 212-228-3895"

The mind reels. Digby's. "This is a gag, right?"

"That's what I thought. I kept telling this Clive person that this is a philosophy magazine. Circulation two thousand. All university types. Maybe there's another *Cogito* somewhere. But he says, No. He knows who we are. Then something about wanting to get in on the ground floor."

"Binx!" Digby yelps.

Madeleine gives him a look that encompasses her current assessment of him, to wit, that he is actually the Tom Hanks character in *Big*, a twelve-year-old outfitted in a middle-aged man's body. She sighs and says, "So how much do we charge them?"

"I have no idea. What did Duke pay?"

"Nine hundred."

"*Dollars?*"

Madeleine indulges the twelve-year-old with a strained smile.

"Maybe I should run this by Mrs. Hastings," Digby says. "What's the product? I mean, what are they advertising?"

"He didn't say."

"Thank you, Madeleine." Digby is feeling so grateful and expansive that he adds, "How's Rosti doing?"

Madeleine pauses, rather dramatically it seems, and replies, "He's definitely on his way."

"Here?"

"Just on his way."

Wending his way back to his office, Digby decides to take the shortcut through the Goldenfield/MacLane bunker—a little high-step strutting seems in order. He does not knock.

"Good morning, Mr. Maxwell."

What is this? A personal greeting from June MacLane— one bordering on cheery?

June is slouched in her computer chair, both hands behind her head. She does not look in Digby's direction, but he can see that there is something resembling a smile on her thin lips. Speaking of which, her upper lip, once the site of several well-tended wiry hairs, is squeaky clean. She has evidently been daydreaming. Now she abruptly snaps to attention and hits the delete button on her computer, but not before Digby can see the headline on her screen: "Baby Boy Names A–Z."

Good God, the woman really is pregnant!

By golly, her condition already seems to be bringing out something unexpectedly womanly—well, at least woman*ish*— in her. Could this have an impact on her feminist *Weltanschauung?* During Digby's stoned crash course on the history of philosophy, he remembers being struck by William James's bizarrely commonsense notion that all metaphysics begins in the gut. Perhaps that includes the womb also.

"Have a good one," Digby calls, exiting through the rear door of her office into his own.

Sitting back in his chair, Digby gazes fondly at the view through his floor-to-ceiling windows.

My domain. Mine, mine, mine.

Among the tulip and daffodil blossoms are some jaunty, bright red gewgaws peeping out here and there. Digby squints. They are vermillion plastic flags flapping atop wooden stakes— boundary markers planted by the sozzled surveyors.

Digby does a little daydreaming himself. He sees Binx Berger holding forth at a Tribeca, hipper-than-hip cocktail party where he lets it be known that he is doing a hilarious piece for this crazy new magazine, *Cogito.* Something between a philosophy journal and *Rolling Stone.* In fact, word has it that it's the new *Rolling Stone* which, as everyone knows, is currently growing moss. It's for today's smarties, the iPad and coke set. But get this—it's burrowing in from the outside, based in some backwoods, white bread college in Vermont. Of course, there's a savvy New Yorker at the helm. Digby Maxwell. Remember him? The middle-aged formerly very-next-thing guy?

Either Saatchi or Saatchi listens raptly to Binx's spiel, taking notes.

Yup, that's undoubtedly how it happened, Digby muses. Old Digby can't help being on the cusp of the very next thing, because the very next thing follows him everywhere he goes. He is about to dial up Felicia Hastings to tell her about his coup of all coups, when he realizes that he doesn't have a clue what product the Saatchi boys plan to push in their full-page ads. Digby needs his ducks all lined up. So he does a few breathing exercises and dials Clive Bosnoglian in New York. Bosnoglian's secretary puts him right through.

"Maxwell. Thanks for getting back to me so quickly."

"My pleasure, Clive. How are things in the Big Apple?"

"Oh, you know, the same old, same old. Always trying to catch the wave."

"Right."

"Looks like you're riding the wave this time, Maxwell."

Digby is attacked by sudden-onset hyperventilation. He closes his eyes and attempts to decrease his oxygen intake.

"I try," Digby finally says. "So listen, Clive, we're happy to reserve those pages for you, but I need a few details to bring to my board. Just a *pro forma* thing. Like who's your client."

"Duke University Press," Clive says.

Jesus Christ, the whole fucking thing is a prank! Scott or Phil put him up to it. Maybe even Fanny. I have been suckered. I am the fool. Thank God I didn't call Felicia.

"Only kidding," Clive Bosnoglian chuckles. "Just wanted you to know I did my homework. We're thinking back page for Jaguar. First turn, iPad. Inside exit, either Gap or Dewar's. All three targeted copy with a philosophy tie-in. Like somebody on the Jaguar account tossed out, 'Don't put Descartes before the horsepower.' Just a thought, but it is kinda cute, ya think?"

"Adorable," Digby says. He is so relieved that the Saatchi deal is not a prank that he actually does find the horsepower gag kinda cute.

"So when can I have some numbers, Maxwell? Throw in a discount for a year's worth so we can toss that around too. And don't get greedy on us, okay? We know what Duke paid."

"That was before—"

"I know, I know. But you're not *Rolling Stone*. Not yet. We're taking a flyer on you."

"I'll be kind," Digby says. "I'll be back to you ASAP."

After hanging up, Digby sits very quietly and, he believes, maturely, at his desk. He removes a fresh sheet of *Cogito* stationery from the middle drawer and sets it in front of him where he taps on it *allegro non troppo* with his pencil. Then he writes down: "Bk. Cover—$6,000. Insides: $4,500" He taps a few measures more and ups his numbers to $7,500 and $5,500. He looks down upon it and, lo, it is good. Actually, for a magazine with a circulation of 2,000, it is outrageously good.

But hold on, those Saatchi fellows are no fools. If they hear buzz, buzz it is. And if they then call up the editor-in-chief in Vermont, that buzz must be a drum roll. They see the circulation skyrocketing very soon. Say up to twenty-five thousand, maybe twice that, every subscriber in the Jaguar disposable income bracket. Okay then, how about $10,000 and $6,000? It's my last offer.

Hold on, indeed. This news needs to be delivered to Felicia in person. Time for a little stroll to the Hastings manse.

He rises, pockets his ad page estimates, and takes a few steps toward the door when the phone rings.

"Maxwell here," he answers. It is his old *New York Magazine* greeting and he likes the masterly sound of it.

"Hi, Digby. It's Muffy."

"I beg your pardon."

"Muffy. Kim's Muffy."

Digby remains clueless, not to mention impatient. "This is *Cogito* magazine," he says. "How can I help you?"

"Muffy," the woman's voice repeats, more than a hint of haughtiness in her voice. "We met at the Rite of Spring shindig. The one where you executed your famous beer bottle *grand jette*."

"I'm so sorry, Muffy. Lot on my mind at the moment."

"Pas de problem," Ms. Muffy says. Digby imagines Miles "Kim" Herker beaming with pride as his wife drops her Francophile *belle phrases* around their too-small president's house. "I've signed you up for next Thursday's Thursday Morning Club. Faculty club dining room. Ten-ish."

"Great. Is there a dress code?"

"Clothing is optional," Muffy titters. "But we do need to settle on a topic. How does 'Marriage and Morality' sound?"

"Like an oxymoron."

"Oh dear, you are as naughty as they say you are," Muffy laughs.

"Listen, Mrs. Herker, I think you should know that I'm not really a philosopher, just a newspaperman without portfolio."

"*Charmant*," Muffy says. "I'll see you on Thursday. We *are* going to have fun, aren't we?"

"Loads."

Going out the front door, Digby nearly collides with Madeleine. "He's getting faint," she mumbles, gesturing to the black plastic oval in her hand, the mother end of Rosti's monitor. He wishes her Godspeed and lopes on toward the Hastings manse on Hawthorne Street.

Minutes later, he is rapping on the Hastings' front door. No response. He presses the doorbell and hears the chimes tinkle something vaguely ecclesiastical. Still no answer. He cranes his head toward Felicia's driveway—her Lexus is there, but that doesn't tell him much as she often walks to town. He invokes one last chime whilst pressing his nose to the front door window and peering in through the Brussels lace curtain.

Lo and behold, inside he beholds a flurry of kinematics. The body in motion belongs to the mistress of the house, Mrs. Felicia Hastings, and it is clad in only brassiere and panties. He instantly withdraws his face and starts backing toward the steps, but not before he spies another body prancing by in the Victorian vestibule. This one belongs to her silver-topped lawyer and it is stark naked.

Digby gets his ass out of there.

CHAPTER 14

Have any of the great philosophers ever shed much light on the topic of sex? Sure, Freud built his entire motivational shtick on the making of whoopee, but that hardly qualifies as a philosophy—it just arbitrarily prioritizes the sex drive over, say, hunger or the ofttimes compelling urge to take a good bowel movement. And true, St. Augustine went on at length about his battle to maintain his celibacy. Who can forget his Comedy Cellar-worthy quip to God, "Give me chastity, *but not yet.*" As Sylvie might say, his presumed outcome was a foregone conclusion.

But who among the Great Thinkers has ever put his or her finger on how sex alters the course of history? Even Nietzsche's *übermensch* forges history with his pants on. Quoth the imperious German, "It is not a lack of love, but a lack of friendship that makes unhappy marriages."

Right, Friedrich, try telling that one to your marriage counselor.

Speaking of St. Augustine and Sylvie, Digby has noted of late a certain chasteness creeping into *The Unmade Bed*; there seems to be a whole lot more moral wrangling and a whole lot less sex going on between the sheets and, not surprisingly, a consequent drop in her online hits. Could she be warming up for a *Cogito* article of her own?

As Digby bounces into his office, visions of Dewar's ads dancing in his head, not to mention visions of Felicia Hastings and her attorney in *flagrante delicto*, he is greeted by Madeleine. She looks flushed. Beside her stands the Russian logician.

"Good morning, Digby," Madeleine says. "Rosti has something he wants to show you."

"I can't imagine what it is," Digby says. Actually, he would prefer not to imagine what it is.

"He's written an amazing piece for the heaven issue," she says.

Digby studies Madeleine's face, trying to determine what exactly it is that has changed there. Her pert, upturned nose and toothy mouth remain the same, pleasantly plain in a wholesome, outdoorsy way. But her eyes—yes, that's what it is; they have turned from smoky quartz to phosphorescent obsidian. Add in her glowing cheeks and Digby concludes that Ms. Follet is recently of the unmade bed. Obviously with the Russian. Because he now sees that Rosti's eyes, atypically, are focused. Something dramatic has caused him to finally take a gander at the real world, a place that is usually only studied by those flim-flam philosophers known as empiricists.

"It came," Rosti announces, knocking the side of his head.

"Wonderful," Digby replies.

Rosti hands a single sheet of paper to Madeleine who, in turn, rises and hands it to Digby. In toto, the Russian's essay covers one-third of the page:

That One
by
Rostislav Demidov, Ph. D.

There are other possible universes.

The probability that they exist is not calculable.

But if they do exist, the probability of any one of them being more heavenly than our universe is 1 in 2.

So if a greater-than-1 to less-than-infinite number of other universes exists, one is the most heavenly.

That one is Heaven.

"Brilliant!" Digby says, although he has not comprehended a word of it. It does, however, strike him as a perfect balance to Binx Berger's upcoming piece. A cardinal rule in New York magazine publishing is to always make the reader feel very smart and deep before hitting him with a juicy bit of gossip or some puerile humor, which is what the reader wanted in the first place but felt too guilty to indulge in.

"His first draft was in logical symbols, but I made him write it out," Madeleine says.

"I bet he wrote it on the back of a napkin, am I right?"

Madeleine and Rostislav exchange giddy glances and Digby is left to imagine on exactly what he penned his post-coital insight into possible heavenly universes. In any event, this confirms it for Digby: the next issue of *Cogito* will be devoted to the philosophy of sex. He envisions Saatchi & Saatchi doubling their ad buys.

The phone rings and Digby picks up.

"Felicia Hastings," the voice says. It is ice.

"Hello, Felicia. How are you?" Digby decides on the spot not to mention that he recently saw her in her underwear.

"We need to talk," she says. "Now. Here."

"I'll be right over."

So back Digby goes to the Hastings manse. He does not feel lighthearted anymore. Felicia's tone of voice has canceled that. Did she spot him sighting her through the window? Is she blaming the witness for what he witnessed?

Digby does not even need to knock for the door to open this time. Mrs. Hastings is not only fully dressed, but has donned a regal lavender dress with gold accessories. She shows him into the parlor with nary a word. He sits.

"We can't have these obscene advertisements, Mr. Maxwell," she says.

Obscene?

How the hell does she know about this already? From Madeleine, no doubt. Yes, Madeleine must have been extremely busy in the last couple of hours.

"I don't think they're obscene. Not in today's world, Felicia. And that's who we're aiming at. Smart young people. I assume you're talking about the scotch ad."

"All of them. The car, that electronic thing, those vulgar dresses."

"Gap?"

"Exactly."

For the life of him, Digby cannot fathom what is going on here. "Do you have any idea what they'd be willing to pay? We're talking five figures per issue."

"*Cogito* is simply not that kind of enterprise."

Digby is about to remind her that the very reason he was brought in was to change *Cogito's* enterprise, but a little voice inside him warns him not to go there. It is the voice of job panic.

"Are you sure this is what Bonner would want?" he asks. He is being provocative, he knows, but he is grasping at straws here.

"Yes."

"You consulted with him?"

"This morning, in fact."

In your bra and panties? With your naked counselor at your side?

"Well, maybe you can tell me what kind of products would be acceptable," Digby says. "What you and Bonner would approve of. Encyclopedias? Yogurt? Lighting fixtures? These are reasonable people, Felicia. I can talk to them."

Felicia appears somewhat flummoxed by Digby's question. Whatever her agenda may be, she apparently has not thought through all the steps thoroughly, and Digby, it seems, has just executed a canny move in this game, the name and aim of which completely elude him.

"We, uh . . . I will have to get back to you on that," she says. And with that, Digby is dismissed.

An odor follows Digby up Hawthorne Street. It is the smell of the proverbial rat. From whence comes all this uppitiness about *Cogito*'s image? Is Felicia's WASPY sense of propriety suddenly asserting itself in spite of Bonner's fondest hopes for the magazine? When Digby showed her proofs of the articles that had already come in, she had no objection to the radical slant of Chuck's piece, and she found Tommy's pictorial utterly charming. And when Digby informed her that their new contributor, Binx Berger, was the head writer at *Saturday Night Live,* she chortled with approval. But now Gap and iPod are too vulgar for consideration? Nope, Digby is sure something else is at play here. And that without a doubt her nudist companion has something to do with it.

Instinctively, Digby's feet have wended him to Louden Clear's door; they have sensed his thirst. He sits at the bar and orders a Dewar's straight up, drinks it down and orders another. He feels he is now ready to think this thing through with an appropriate lack of clarity. He lines up ducks in the form of swizzle sticks:

Duck #1: Felicia Hastings has a lover.

Duck #2: Her lover is her lawyer.

Duck #3: There's a distinct chance that said lover was in the picture before her husband died.

Duck #4: They were not pleased by Saatchi & Saatchi's offer to buy ads, saying that the products were inappropriate.

Duck #5: That reason sounds like baloney.

Digby downs his second scotch in one gulp. He considers the ducks from his new, two-Dewar's perspective. Obviously, Felicia and Silver Fox want something. He calls that 'X' because he doesn't know what it is.

Winny walks in the door with a bag full of groceries.

Now where was I? 'X'?

"Love problems?" Winny says, setting her groceries on top of Digby's carefully lined-up ducks.

"Not mine."

Winny sits on the stool next to Digby's. "You're getting soused over somebody else's love life? Mine, for example?"

Digby laughs. It is actually good to see Winny. He had been feeling lonely, as one will when drinking alone in the afternoon.

"Felicia Hastings' love life," Digby says recklessly.

"With Ronald, you mean?"

"Is that her lawyer?"

"Nobody's ever seen his diploma, but that's what he says he is."

"How long have they been an item?"

"You mean before or after Bonner's demise?" Winny asks. She signals the barman for a beer and a refill of Digby's glass.

"Yup."

"The common wisdom is before."

"Was he Bonner's lawyer too?"

"Good question." Their drinks arrive; they execute a mug and scotch glass clink. "Apparently Ronald applied for the job, but Bonner stuck with his old lawyer to the end. Bob Baskerton, a townie." Winny gives Digby a little neck rub that is too comforting to resist. "Why the interest? You don't have designs on her too, do you?"

Digby offers Winny a drinker's look of suffering and contriteness, guilt and its excuse rolled into one soulful side glance.

"She's acting funny," Digby says.

"Geriatric sex will do that to a person," Winny says. It occurs to Digby that Sylvie might do well to sign up Winny as a consulting editor. "Rumor has it that they're planning their escape from Louden. Palm Beach."

"Sounds good to me. Everybody should live happily ever after."

"But apparently it's not that easy to make Ronald happy. He has expensive tastes in real estate."

"Do we suspect Ronald of being an opportunist?" Digby asks.

"Funny word," Winny says. She offers Digby another in the standard lexicon of drinker's looks, this one combining world weariness with resignation. In context, it says, '*all* men are opportunists,' so Digby keeps his trap shut.

"I didn't think you were that interested in local gossip," she says after a moment.

"I guess I have too much time on my hands."

Winny responds with another neck rub. Her hands are still on Digby's neck when two more afternoon customers walk into Louden Clear—Mary Bonavitacola and June MacLane. Digby ignores his impulse to shrug off Winny's hand.

"Hi," Mary says to both of them. She and June keep walking until they reach a booth at the far wall.

"So, how's your romance with the parson going?" Winny says, giving Digby's neck a final squeeze.

"It's strictly spiritual."

"What a shame," Winny says mockingly, but at this point Digby is barely listening. He is gazing across the room to where Mary has reached across the table and is maternally patting June's belly.

"Sweet," Winny croons. "I wonder what they'll name him."

"*They?*"

Winny flashes Digby an unambiguous smile: it is a smile of triumph. And then she picks up her bag of groceries and leaves.

Trapdoors.
All over the fucking place.
You were right, Mr. Schopenhauer, hopefulness is just a setup for a ruinous fall in this, the worst of all possible worlds.

CHAPTER 15

In fact, Arthur Schopenhauer did not consider himself a pessimist; he thought of himself as a realist, if believing that the entire universe is an illusion can be considered realism, which Professor Schopenhauer did. He was one of the first in Europe to read the teachings of the Buddha and apparently the sound of one hand clapping resonated with him. Echoing the Buddha, Schopenhauer stated that since the whole deal is one big illusion, the ups and downs along the way do not amount to a hill of beans. This actually can be a very comforting philosophy, especially during periods when shit is making repeated contact with the fan.

Digby is more than ready to accept the universe as illusory by the time he returns from Louden Clear to his apartment. In fact, he yearns for that region of full-immersion illusion known as Fool's Paradise. But he needs a nudge to get there, so he supplements the stupefaction of his afternoon scotches with the mind-body dissociation of a joint. For obvious reasons, all resolutions of character improvement have been called off.

But chemistry alone does not do the trick; his mind, though seriously whacked, keeps returning to Mary's affectionate tap of June's womb, and to Felicia Hastings' maddening and inscrutable ad nixing. He needs further distraction, so he snaps on his TV.

Playing there is the film, *What Dreams May Come*, featuring the mind-numbing actor, Robin Williams, on a Cook's tour of paradise. Digby had started viewing the film a few days earlier as part of his private heaven-in-the-movies film festival in preparation for his article on same. Before the trapdoors started flopping open in front of him, Digby had been feeling so smart and peppy that he gave the assignment to himself. Who better than droll old Digby? The film action picks up where Digby left off several days ago with the Robin Williams character, who has just arrived in paradise, meeting his old pooch. Says Robin, "Boy, I screwed up. I'm in dog heaven."

It only gets worse. The heaven in *What Dreams May Come* is depressingly gloopy. The color scheme is Renoir on LSD. Doggies fly. Flowers do the hoochie coochie. Rainbows swirl like kite tails. Robin thinks it's divine. Digby, on the other hand, is convinced that Eternal Nothingness would be a far better option. He finally clicks off the television set. He lies down on his bed and places the telephone on his chest.

Digby is dialing Mary's number knowing full well that her answering machine will pick up. The reason he knows this is because he just dialed her number two minutes ago. And two minutes before that. He is now just sober enough to know that this constitutes compulsive behavior; but he is also just stoned enough to know that compulsive behavior is justified when you have recently learned that the woman with whom you just may happen to be in love is in some kind of consensual relationship with another woman who happens to be pregnant.

Mary's answering machine picks up. She probably has caller-ID. This time, the moment he hangs up, his phone rings. *Mary has had second thoughts!*

"Hello?"

"Hi!" *Is* it Mary? Digby tries to concentrate.

"Good to hear from you," he says.

"Dad, are you stoned?" Digby's daughter.

"Of course not, Sylvie." The new world order where middle-class parents lie to their children about their drug habits.

"You sound funny," Sylvia says.

"I try."

"Listen, I've got some major news."

"I'm all ears."

"I'm getting married."

Digby's concentration momentarily splinters. *Who is getting married? Mary? To June?*

"Congratulations," he says, recomposing. "Who's the lucky . . ."

"Ahmed. He's a professor. Statistics. We met online."

"A, uh, a dating service?"

"You're so old-fashioned, Dad."

"I've begun to realize that lately."

"Ahmed was a fan of *The Unmade Bed*. He wrote comments every day. Plot ideas. One thing led to another."

"Life imitates art."

"Actually, I'm selling my half of the site."

"Your half of the bed, so to speak."

"Whatever. The wedding's in June. Corny, huh? You're invited, by the way."

"I'm honored, Sylvie. Do I get to give away the bride?"

"Not really. It's a Muslim ceremony."

Full sobriety is staging a comeback, but along with it comes the overwhelming feeling that Digby is adrift in an unfamiliar universe. "Is your mother coming?"

"Of course. Jesus, that's not a problem for you, is it?"

"Not at all. Men and women sit separately in a mosque anyhow, right?"

"It's not in a mosque, Dad. It's at the Palo Alto Hills Country Club."

"Sounds delightful."

"And don't worry, Mom and Phil are paying for it."

"Phil?"

"*Duh*-uh. Her husband."

Digby is at a loss for words.

"You didn't know?" Sylvie says. Digby thinks he even detects a trace of mercy in her voice.

"I have a pile of unread email," he says lamely. "Is he nice? This Phil. Have you met him?"

"They came out to visit. Phil Weinstein. You know him, right?"

"It doesn't ring a bell."

"He used to be Phil Winston, but he changed it back to his grandfather's name. It's an identity thing."

Phil Winston? Phil Winston the shmuck?

"I worked for a guy by that name at the *Voice*. But it's probably a common name."

"No, that's the guy," Sylvia says. "He told me he was an old friend of yours."

Digby laughs. Even Schopenhauer would have a good giggle at this.

"What's funny about that?" Sylvia asks.

"I'm laughing with happiness," he says. "For Mom. Mom and Phil."

Actually, this is only partially true. Another reason he is laughing is he now sees Phil Winston-Weinstein in a new light—as a man who will save him alimony payments.

"All is good in God's heaven," Digby says.

"Are you being sarcastic?"

"Not at all. I couldn't be happier for you, Sylvie. I mean that. I hope you are very happy. Give my best to Ahmed." Much to Digby's surprise and pleasure, he really does mean every word of it.

"Okay." Sylvia sounds bewildered by her father's generosity of spirit.

Jesus, do I come off as that uncharitable to her most of the time? Digby experiences a spasm of parental guilt that convinces him he deserves to fall through every trapdoor from here to eternity.

After a moment, Digby says, "Guess I'll stop reading *The Unmade Bed*."

"It was getting boring anyhow, right?"

"Well, there *was* more talk and less turnover," Digby says, then adds, "I was starting to miss the statistical element." He immediately regrets this last; he doesn't wish to cast any aspersions on her intended's profession. But thankfully Sylvie laughs. Goodbye, goodbye. Digby curls up on his bed, closes his eyes, and the phone rings.

"Sylvie?"

"I guess we need to talk." *Mary!*

Digby makes himself a strong mug of *Camellia sinensis*; he needs utter clarity for his conversation with Mary. He follows that with a cold shower, dresses in fresh shirt and pants, and heads out into the lukewarm night.

At one in the morning, illuminated by a half-moon, the streets of Louden are calendar picturesque: the New England village is asleep, at peace. On the other hand, the vacant streets also look embalmed, like they have been hit by a neutron bomb. "There are no facts, only interpretations," to quote Mary's T-shirt.

Instead of devoting the next issue of *Cogito* to sex, how about going all the way and making it about love? The Oxford linguistic philosophers say that 'love' is the vaguest denotation in the lexicon, that at best it is just a reflexive response on the same order as reacting to an itch. So why all this poetry about love making the world go 'round? More to the point, how is a middle-aged man supposed to know if he really has fallen in love with a woman with whom he has only rendezvoused a handful of times; or if he is so far gone that he wouldn't know love if it hit him in the face like a pasta fazool?

Mary awaits Digby in the doorway of the Universalist Unitarian Church wearing a loose-fitting jogging outfit that looks like it sometimes doubles as sleepwear. The moonlight is just bright enough for Digby to make out next Sunday's sermon title on the placard in the window: **"But Seriously, Folks— Isn't Life Just a Big Joke?"**

"I'm making tea," she greets him. "You want?"

"Yes, thank you."

Moments later they are sitting across from one another at a small, drop-leaf table in the pastor's study which, apparently, is also her bedroom—a futon covered by a patchwork comforter lies beside the far wall. They both sip tea silently for a moment.

"I still haven't figured out why I need to tell you this," she begins. "At the very least I didn't want you to hear about it from anybody else. But telling you—telling you now—doesn't mean anything more than just telling you, if that makes any sense."

Digby nods. He is now as sober as Thomas De Quincey. He is also shaky.

"Okay, here goes. Reuben—my husband. No, *both* of us wanted to have children. Well, one, at least."

Digby nods again.

"But there were problems. In my uterus. Fibroid things. Every time I conceived, it wouldn't hold. Nowhere for it to attach to the wall. So the next step was to conceive in a test tube, scrape me clean, and then attach the little bugger fast before the fibroids grew back." She smiles weakly and Digby returns the smile just as weakly.

"Then just after we completed step one—the test tube— Reuben was diagnosed with pancreatic cancer. A death sentence. They put the embryo in the freezer and that was that."

Mary stops. She looks forlorn and all Digby wants to do is hug her, pat her hair, and tell her that everything is going to be all right, but he has no idea if that is what she wants or needs, so he just says, "Go on when you're ready, okay?"

"I lied in my sermon," she says, looking straight at Digby. "In my article for you too. I mean, about those last days together on the Cape. I left out a crucial part. Reuben and I weren't silent all the time we watched those sunsets. We talked. A lot. We talked about what in the name of God happens next. Neither of us believed in heaven or any other kind of afterlife. And that Eternal Now thing? Well, it really was incredibly beautiful, truly transcendental—I didn't lie about that. But it didn't do the trick, you know? Not in lived time. Not for a man who was going to die in a few days with a whole lot of his life still unlived."

"I can understand that," Digby says.

"The only option he could believe in was, you know, the chain of life. He was a mathematician and he had a mathematical term for what he meant—something called the continuum hypothesis."

"He wanted you to have his baby."

"Yup."

"So you promised him you would."

"I tried to promise him, but he wouldn't accept it. He said it was stupid and selfish of him and it wouldn't make any difference anyhow because he would be dead. 'Eternally dead,' as he put it."

"But you wanted to keep that promise anyhow."

"Yes, I did. But it didn't turn out to be so easy. Medically, I mean. New problems in my uterus, complications."

"I think I know the rest," Digby says softly to her.

"Just part of the rest, Digby. Finding a surrogate to carry the baby and June volunteering for the job. I guess you know that part."

"There's more?"

"Yes."

Then Mary starts to weep. At first, it is just a little catch in her throat but then, before she turns her head away from Digby, tears form in the corners of her eyes and begin to slide down her flushed cheeks. This time Digby allows his instincts to prevail; he stands and walks to her, places his hands gently on her shuddering shoulders, and whispers, "It's okay, friend. It's okay." Meaningless words, words of comfort are; they are on a par with 'love' for nebulousness. But the thing is, they are the best the heart has in its vocabulary.

"I'm an asshole!" Mary cries out.

"Please, Mary."

She straightens up and Digby treads softly back to his seat.

"No, honestly. I'm a total asshole," Mary says, now back in control of her voice. "For starters, I hate the whole surrogate womb business. It's like a modern version of a wet nurse. Leaving the icky part of childbearing to the servants."

"It sounds like you didn't have any choice in the matter."

"It still rankles. But that's hardly the worst of it."

"Something about June," Digby says.

"Yes, June. We've been friends ever since Reuben and I moved up here. She's a good person, you know. Like everybody else, she puts on a good show of being a tough cookie, but it's not easy for her."

"Being gay?"

"All the gender philosophy in the world doesn't do a bit of good when you go home for Thanksgiving to a family of Baptists."

Digby knows whereof Mary speaks from his bit of shameless eavesdropping. Again he nods.

"She was wonderful to me after Reuben died. Understanding, comforting. She virtually moved in and took care of me."

"And you told her about your promise to Reuben."

"To myself! My promise to myself!" Mary snaps, then, "I'm sorry. But I always need to remember that. Reuben absolutely refused my pledge. He said it wasn't fair. Not fair at all. The fact is he died thinking I wasn't going to go through with it, so it's all mine now. My decision."

"Okay."

"I need to walk," Mary says.

They head out into the night, Mary leading the way. No words now. Blessed silence. She takes them to the edge of town where a thick spruce forest announces the first rise of the mountains. Mary points to the sky.

"That is still the biggest comfort in the universe to me," she says quietly. "The smallness of my life. The speckiness of it." She laughs. "Not very profound, am I?"

"But seriously, folks," Digby says.

Mary laughs again, squeezes his arm, then lets go and sits on a large rock under a spreading spruce.

"There's a lot of legal higgledy-piggledy you have to go through to arrange for a surrogate pregnancy," she says. "We had a local lawyer handle it. Bob Baskerton."

Bonner Hastings' attorney, as Digby recently learned. "Was he up to it? Doesn't sound like a common item in a small town practice."

"Bob did his homework. There aren't that many variables. Payments for care of the surrogate, obstetric bills, that sort of thing. And then there's the nitty-gritty, like does the surrogate get any visiting rights?"

"Sounds like it could get tricky." Digby sits down on the rock also, but with his back to hers. Their relative positions feel like they will make this conversation easier, as if their words will have to patiently circumnavigate the Earth to reach one another.

"It didn't seem so at the time," Mary goes on. "June and I are good friends, we live in the same town. Bob—Bob Baskerton—said we should think about it carefully. One of us might move away, that sort of thing. But we said we could work it out if something like that came up, so we checked the box for 'full visiting rights.'"

Digby pauses a moment before he says, "I have a confession to make."

His words circle the globe and Mary says, "Go ahead."

"I overheard June talking to her mother at the office. I didn't have a clue that you were involved at that point. June said to her mother, 'We're having a baby.' I thought she was talking about a girlfriend, her partner, whoever that was. That they were having a baby together. She didn't sound like some dispassionate surrogate."

Mary is crying in earnest now. She leans back on the rock, her spine against his. In the moment, it feels more intimate than a coital embrace. After a while she manages to say, "I didn't see it coming."

"I'm sure you didn't."

"I should have!" Mary cries. "I didn't want to see it, so I didn't. I probably even encouraged it, goddamn it! It happened little by little, you know? I'd pat her belly and say things like, 'How's our little guy doing today?' *Our* little guy! Before I knew it, she was talking about what we were going to feed him and where our little guy would go to nursery school. It got out of hand, way out of hand, and I didn't do anything to stop it. I *don't* do anything to stop it!"

They remain silent for a long while. Clearly, Mary made a terrible mistake the moment she elected to borrow June's womb. Everything that followed germinated from that heedless seed. They both know that. 'No blame,' as it says in the *I Ching*. There is nothing more to say about it. But Digby needs to say something to Mary now, something—anything—that will give her some peace.

"We'll find a way to make it work" is what he says.

"Don't!" Mary's back stiffens against his. "I don't want you to do anything, Digby!"

"Sorry," he murmurs. "I didn't mean—" But, of course, Digby did mean exactly what he said, that somehow he could be a part of helping her through this, that somehow he *hopes* he can be a part of helping her through this.

They remain seated back to back on the rock. Slowly her spine relaxes into Digby's again and they stay that way for several minutes. Then they walk back to the church. At the door, she says, "I'm sorry, Digby. I didn't even say a word about this craziness that you're going through with Felicia Hastings."

"Hey, it's not that big a deal," Digby says, and at the moment it really does not feel like one to him.

Mary gives him a quick peck on the cheek and disappears inside her church.

CHAPTER 16

What lingers from Digby's Bleecker Street game of "Me Too" is the feeling that if becoming someone else is so easily accomplished, being himself is strictly arbitrary—a chance occurrence on the same order as a hummingbird opting for the nectar of Hollyhock 'A' instead of Hollyhock 'B.' This can be a supremely liberating feeling. Digby does possess an ego, of course, and it seems determined to make something out of him, but he does not really think very highly of his ego. For one thing, not to put too fine a point on it, it is egotistical.

The entire idea of the individual man with a self and a soul and an idiosyncratic list of personal characteristics and styles turns out to be a relatively recent historical development, and Digby is starting to think humankind took an unwise turn when they forsook group identity for the whole one-man, one-destiny path. For starters, it is altogether lonelier. Like the individual man dies alone. Now *that* is lonely.

It sounds to Digby as if Reuben was trying to reach for some kind of transpersonal immortality with his so-called 'continuum hypothesis,' to wit, living on through his kid. Never mind that his kid will have no memory of his father, let alone some kind of inborn consciousness of being an extension of him. But maybe Reuben was after bigger game here, something more abstract and spooky, more like immortality through the survival of his tribe, his herd. But why stop there? Why not reach for immortality through the Family of Man, where Han Wing's son in Taipei or Sven Langstrom's son in Stockholm would be enough to do the trick for him? Hey, why even stop there? Survival of all God's creatures, great and small. Throw in the plant kingdom while you're at it. Or maybe go the whole route—the survival of Being itself!

Such are Digby's surprisingly philosophical thoughts as he treads up Brigham Street on his way to the Thursday Morning Club. He has slept in his clothes and badly, emotionally exhausted after returning home from his late night rendezvous with Mary.

Except for the sherry, broccoli florets, and onion dip, the Thursday Morning Club looks alarmingly like Dr. Epstein's therapy group: a ring of folding chairs upon which comely ladies sit, albeit comely ladies of a certain age. Digby has arrived rumpled and unprepared. In fact, it is not until Muffy Herker introduces him—"our very own New York *literatus*"—and announces the topic of the day—"marriage and morals"—that he recalls his assigned duties.

Standing in the center of their circle, tucking in an errant shirttail, he feels like he is about to partake in an ancient rite, the Ritual Stoning of the Malevolent Male. No doubt, he deserves it. Instinctively, he folds his arms in front of him for protection.

"The bilateral marriage is a relatively new phenomenon and it is already going out of date. It has outlived its usefulness," Digby begins, recalling his own state of mind when he and Fanny separated. "Anthropologically, marriage is a corporate institution. Shared dwelling and food, shared childcare. Mutual benefits. Pure economics. So questions of morality are identical to those of any corporation. Do costs outnumber benefits? Is each party fulfilling his or her assigned role? Carrying its load?"

Digby is on a roll. He is just starting to believe that he actually is a New York litterateur, when he gazes up at his audience. They appear disappointed. Bored, in fact. He can tell that by the way they are playing with their broccoli florets. Part of him doesn't give a rat's ass, but another part of him is back at Epstein's group sessions, wanting more than anything to amuse the ladies.

"Of course, a fundamental part of this corporate deal has to do with sex," he goes on, hoping that this segue will garner more interest. "Who gets it and, more importantly, who doesn't. It's the 'who doesn't' part that gets dicey. Because the deal is that each party will abstain from diddling anyone else."

Attention is paid. Raptly. Florets are stilled. Panty-girdled bottoms edge forward on seats. It is a thrill to be thrilling. Digby can't help himself.

"To put it simply, monogamy is unnatural. God forgive us, we aren't built that way. To quote the philosopher, Lenny Bruce, 'In certain circumstances, men will fuck mud.'"

Titters. Digby adores titters. He surveys his audience. Faculty wives all, he is sure. They are all elegantly coiffed and impeccably decked out in classic garments—from the local Talbots, if he is not mistaken. Here and there a patch of upper sternum is exposed, but no cleavage in sight. Yet the air is redolent with pheromones. Sex glistens on their painted lips. Digby is now quite certain that the Thursday Morning Club is heavily populated with horny ladies. This, of course, raises the question of what they expect from him. Could this be an ancient ritual involving a different kind of male sacrifice?

"Women are no different from men in this regard," he goes on blithely. "It is now accepted fact that women's sexual appetites exceed those of men, especially as time and marriages go on. Add to this the fact that modern contraception techniques have rendered the old, 'Who's your daddy?' question obsolete, and the corporate sexual model crumbles. The only question that remains is, 'What difference does a little extramarital hanky-panky make?' And the answer is, 'Not much.' Or possibly, 'What you don't know won't hurt you.'"

Digby blathers on for a few more minutes, the temperature in the room rising perceptibly. Does he see here and there a lascivious tongue protruding from pursed lips? Is the reason he is straining to aspirate his vowels because the air is thick with estrogen? Is he willing to make the ultimate sacrifice? It *would* take his mind off the rash of mayhem that lately has been spreading over the corpus of his life.

He finishes up with the old Ten Commandments gag: "Moses comes down from the mountain and says to the multitude, 'I have good news and bad news. The good news is I got Him down to ten. The bad news is adultery is still in.'"

A standing, heavy-breathing ovation. Muffy signals Digby to remain at the center of the circle. He notes that it was prescient of him to wear rumpled, casual wear—it can simply be tossed in the garbage after they rip it from his trembling torso.

"I am sure Mr. Maxwell will be happy to answer any questions," Muffy says.

Mr. Maxwell awaits the onslaught. A hand is raised.

"Mr. Maxwell, when Jane Austen wrote, 'Happiness in marriage is entirely a matter of chance,' what was she implying?"

Digby is stunned. Chagrined. Stupefied. Jane Austen, for Christ's sake? He gazes around at the smiling faces. They all suddenly look Stepford-like. He retakes the room's temperature. It has tumbled way down, now just above chilling. Either they have reverted to type or his imagination has been on a binge again.

"My most optimistic interpretation of Ms. Austen's remark is that she thought marriage is what you make of it," he drones in reply.

"Thank you, Mr. Maxwell."

The next question is—honest to God—"Do you think marriage is a sacrament?"

At that moment Digby realizes what has been going on here. They came for titillation and titters, a cerebral Chippendales routine, but that is all. His mildly transgressive and gently smutty commentary on marriage and morals will carry them gleefully through their lackluster week until next Thursday morning's meeting. Who will be their next guest lecturer, the local gynecologist? Digby feels more soiled than if they *had* torn off his clothes and had their way with him.

"Yes, definitely a sacrament," he says. "I'm afraid I have to leave now. Late for a meeting, you know."

Digby is jogging by the time he reaches Brigham Street. He does not feel well. He feels nausea of the Sartrean variety and he thinks he knows what the problem is: his Unique Self is trying to make a comeback. It is Mary's doing. His feelings for her do not want to be spread around among the hollyhocks. It is an 'I and Thou' thing: Digby does not want to be anybody else while loving her.

Without thinking, he has rambled all the way to the rock under the spreading spruce tree upon which Mary and he built their church of intimacy last night. He sits, catching his breath. Then, unbidden, an insight descends from the heavens and it is a whopper: his slippery soul and his inability to take himself seriously are cut from the same piece of cloth. If he does not own his own self, he can keep gliding blithely through life; but he will not love anyone completely and that is a loss of vast proportions.

I finally get it, Dr. Epstein. I am in serious trouble. I am also seriously in love for the first time in my life.

Before Digby can fully inspect his epiphany, he is distracted by a twig snap behind him. Twenty feet away, he sees Rosti the logician duck behind a fallen tree trunk. Then, from Digby's left, he hears a woman's voice call, "It's beeping faster! I'm getting warmer." It takes Digby a moment to identify this as Madeleine's voice because she has tricked it up with the coy, sing-songy tones of a schoolgirl. Madeleine and Rosti are apparently playing a game of high-tech hide-and-seek. Digby slips off the rock, hides behind a thick spruce, and watches as the pair stumble about giggling and squealing until finally the huntress leaps at the hunted and tackles him to the ground. Digby sneaks away before he has to witness the kill.

Back on Brigham Street, the air is cool and sweet. Digby breathes deep, again and again. In front of Hastings Towers he gazes at the little flags atop the surveyor's stakes as they flicker among newly bloomed tulips. It occurs to him that he could see these as flags of distress, but he could just as well see them as banners of renewal. "There are no facts, only interpretations." Digby seems to be quoting Nietzsche via Mary's T-shirt regularly these days.

And then, unexpectedly, the finale of his epiphany descends on him. It is both utterly banal and crystal clear: *Love actually is what makes the world go 'round.*

CHAPTER 17

Digby must have dipped in and out of Uncommon Grounds for double lattes scores of times without noticing the shingle over the shop's adjacent door. It says, "Robert Baskerton, LLB" and Attorney Baskerton is Digby's destination this morning.

Digby opens the door and ascends the stairs. Baskerton shares the second floor with an ophthalmologist and a Reiki master or, in this case, a Reiki mistress, the proprietress being one Lily Spencer. The top half of the lawyer's door is frosted glass bearing his name in black letters, Spade-and-Archer-like. It is ajar, but Digby knocks anyhow.

"Come on in," a voice calls out.

Digby enters. A portly fellow in his seventies or eighties with a ruddy, heavily lined face is sitting at a Louis XV desk upon which sits a Hammond Multiplex typewriter. He says, "Don't mind if I don't get up, I'd only have to sit down again."

"Mr. Baskerton?"

"The only one left," he says. "What can I do you for?"

He gestures to the leather wingback across from him and Digby sits. "My name is Digby Maxwell. The new editor of Bonner Hastings' magazine," he says.

Baskerton lets loose a wheezy horse laugh. "So you're the patsy, eh?" he says.

"Beg pardon?"

"The gull. The chump," he says by way of clarification.

"Are you referring to me?"

Baskerton offers Digby an amiable smile. "I wondered how long it would be before you paid me a call."

"Was it sooner or later than you expected?"

"Just about on time," he says. "Considering you're a New Yorker."

"That would make me some kind of naïf, I suppose."

"It's all relative, as Mr. Einstein said to his grandmother," says Baskerton.

Digby is already developing a fondness for this man. He has always had a weakness for grade school humor.

"May I ask, sir, why you were expecting me?"

"Because nobody, no matter how tough-skinned, likes to play the fool."

"And that's what I've been doing?"

"Not on purpose, Mr. Maxwell. I hear you are a funny man, but not foolish."

"I'll take that as a compliment," Digby says. After yesterday's Thursday Morning Club, chatting with Baskerton feels as fresh and droll as lunch at the Algonquin roundtable. "Exactly what kind of fool have I been playing? Does it have anything to do with Felicia Hastings' relationship to her counselor?"

"Counselor? That must be the kindest honorific anybody ever stuck on Ronald LeFevre since he moved to town."

"He has bad intentions?"

"'Bad' is another one of those relatives, like Einstein's grandma. But LeFevre has intentions all right. They include oceanfront real estate and hot and cold running chambermaids."

"So I've heard. But where does the fool come in? Me, that is."

"Is it too soon before lunch to have an after-dinner drink, Mr. Maxwell?"

"Possibly too late. You can call me Digby, if you want."

Baskerton pulls open a drawer of his desk and removes a bottle of Courvoisier and two snifters. He pours, they clink. "The fool doth think he is wise, but the wise man knows himself a fool," he says by way of a toast.

This country lawyer appears to be the most entertaining man in Louden, Vermont, including the entire faculty of its eponymous college. Digby sniffs, rolls it around in his mouth, and swallows a delicious swig of brandy. "I think I can take it now," he says.

"I wouldn't be too sure of that, Mr. Maxwell. It's on the high end of the mind-boggling scale."

"Boggle me."

"Okay, you asked for it. Louden College in general and Kim Herker in particular have designs on Hastings Towers," Baskerton begins. "Everybody knows that, possibly even you."

Digby nods in the affirmative.

"But as long as *Cogito* lives on, the Towers continue to exist in the Hastings trust." Baskerton grins. "That sounds like one of those philosophy axioms, doesn't it? Descartes or somebody."

Digby smiles appreciatively and Baskerton continues. "But here's the tricky part—once the magazine goes belly up, Felicia is not only free to sell the real estate, she gets the trust money that's been keeping the magazine afloat."

Digby sips some more brandy to steady himself. He senses the mind-boggling part coming on.

"So along about the time Bonner had his first stroke, Felicia turned up here with a little codicil to his will to the effect that if annual circulation of the magazine drops below eight hundred and/or ad revenues drop below five hundred dollars, *Cogito* goes bust. Of course, it didn't smell right to me, so I paid a private visit to Bonner and he assured me he approved it, and he seemed *compos mentis* enough to me. He said that if that many people lost interest in philosophy, the magazine should be doomed with them. But he didn't believe for a minute it would happen. Not one minute. He simply couldn't imagine losing that many ads or subscribers. He called them part of the *Cogito* family. Loyal to the end. He even quipped that they'd follow him anywhere. He was right about that— they followed him into the grave. Bonner's corpse was still warm when your main advertiser snuffed out too—pulled its ads, that is."

"Duke Press," Digby says.

"Exactly. Duke Press has owned the back page of *Cogito* since Bonner started the magazine."

"For all of seven hundred dollars. That's hardly a major investment."

"It was symbolic to Bonner. People who are born with money get goose bumps from earning seven hundred dollars all by themselves. But mostly he saw it as an affirmation of his magazine. A seven-hundred-dollar vote of confidence."

"But apparently Duke took the money seriously. Otherwise they wouldn't have pulled their page from my heaven issue."

"Let's just say they didn't have to feel bad about pulling it. And that's because you, Mr. Maxwell, are *not* family. I've got to give it to that LeFevre, he's sly as a fox and twice as hairy."

"How much is Louden willing to pay for the Towers?"

"One million dollars."

"That seems excessive."

"Not when you look at what the idiot parents are willing to pay for a Louden College education. Fifty thousand a year. Two hundred grand for a Bachelor of Arts. As far as I can tell, for that sum their kids still come out of there without the ability to construct a single comprehensible sentence."

"But they can Tweet."

Baskerton groans and refills their snifters.

"Let me get this straight. Are you saying that the reason I was hired was to run the magazine into the ground?" Digby asks.

"Yup. And from what I hear, you're doing a pretty good job of it."

"Thank you. But I don't get it. That can't be what Bonner wanted."

"Absolutely not. He loved that magazine as only a sterile old man can love the seeds of his mind. It was the only immortality available to him."

Clearly, Bob Baskerton is also the most talented metaphorist in a hundred mile radius.

"I'm still missing something here," Digby says. "So why wouldn't Bonner want the magazine to stay exactly the way it was? His little family was happy—Duke, his subscribers. Why mess with a good thing?"

"Why, indeed? Last I heard Bonner was even grooming Elliot Goldenfield to take over for him. Goldenfield was the man's walking footnote. Elliot wouldn't have changed the magazine a whit. You came as a surprise to everybody."

"Really? That's hard to believe considering Bonner's deathbed request that *Cogito* go pop. Philosophy for the masses."

"I heard about that," Baskerton says. "Total fabrication."

That does it: Digby's mind boggles seismographically. For a master bullshitter, he turns out to be as naïve as a tulip when it comes to the complex cunning of these Louden professionals.

"Jesus! Felicia made up that whole bedside business?"

"Every word of it. With a little help from her friend."

"Holy shit!" Digby's brandy-illuminated brain connects the remaining dots. "But then I fucked up their plans."

"Really? How so?"

Digby tells Baskerton about Binx Berger, *Cogito's* New York buzz, Saatchi & Saatchi's ad bid, and Felicia blowing off their offer.

Upon hearing this flakey twist of fate, Baskerton howls so hard he finally has to rest his forehead on his desk a few moments before speaking again. "So the worm turned and he turned out to be a marketing genius. How did you generate this so-called buzz, Mr. Maxwell?"

"I have my hand on the pulse of America."

"And the other one up your ass."

"Precisely."

"Mine, too," says Baskerton. "I'm not a suspicious man by nature, an unfortunate trait for a lawyer. So I didn't even blink when I saw that as executive publisher of *Cogito*, Mrs. Hastings could reject any advertisement she deemed unworthy.

Maybe this LeFevre fella never went to law school, but he thinks like F. Lee Bailey. He covered every exit."

They sip in silence for a few seconds, then Baskerton says, "Nothing would make me happier than hoisting that LeFevre by his own petard. That's French for fart, you know. Petard."

There is a knock at the door. Baskerton calls, "Come on in," and on in come a dour-faced young couple, the man in jeans and a khaki shirt, the woman in a waitress uniform. Digby's guess is that they've come to divide up their joint property, such as it is, and he finds himself aching for them. A half hour with Baskerton and he is feeling strangely humane. He rises to leave.

"I'll be thinking, petard-wise," Digby says. "Any help would be appreciated."

"Glad you stopped by, Maxwell," says Baskerton. "I needed a little poke to get my mind working again. Sloth is bad for an old man's health."

CHAPTER 18

Digby is walking up Brigham Street with a surprising lightness of foot; once again, in a period of less than two months in Louden, Vermont, he is tasting a bittersweet morsel of existential freedom. He should be wholly enraged after hearing Baskerton's tale of Mrs. Hastings' connivery, especially its obvious implication that the time has come for Digby to pack his bags. Yet finally discerning the pattern of Felicia's deviousness brings him a dulcet dose of peace. He can only take so much of viewing the world through a glass darkly—or through a front door window starkly, for that matter—before he starts to fall apart. Give me clarity or give me claret, as Chuck Jones used to say.

Wasn't that how philosophy came into existence in the first place? Because some jittery Greek—Thales of Miletus, was it?—could not stand another minute of murky-mindedness? He probably was on his knees in his backyard, rocking his classical head in his hands, and yelling into the void: "Hey, I don't mind if Truth stinks—I just need a big dose of it and I need it fast. Otherwise my head is going to explode."

There is another reason why Digby is feeling happier than should be expected under his present circumstances. It is this vision of himself as a man with his bags packed. Bob Dylan must have been reading Schopenhauer when he wrote, "When you've got nothing, you've got nothing to lose." Digby's vision brings on that old, stranger-in-town feeling and that feeling draws him into the Here and Now, a place and time of unparalleled vividness.

"I nailed him!" a voice behind Digby bellows.

Digby turns to behold President Kim Herker in full jogger regalia—a Louden College-emblazened T-shirt and sweat pants, and drooping white sweat socks that reveal surprisingly fragile-looking ankles above his Air Jordans. He is jogging heavily toward Digby who instinctively braces himself, fearing a sweat-bearing bear hug or worse, one of those NBA chest bumps.

"I force myself to do this twice a day," Herker says, pulling up alongside Digby. He laughs. "They say a run a day keeps the bogeyman away. Well, you don't see any bogeymen here in Louden, do you, Maxwell?"

Chuck Jones once did a piece for Digby at *New York Magazine* about Michael Jackson's racial ambiguity in which that word, 'bogeyman,' figured prominently. According to Chuck, the term comes to us by way of the German, *Der schwarze Mann*—the black man—so he deemed bogeyman a racist term regardless of whether the people who used it knew its origin. At the time, Digby had told Chuck that he had gone too far this time, crossing over the line into racial paranoia. But now, hearing the word issue from Herker's mouth, Digby reconsiders Chuck's position.

"Keeps the old blood flowing, eh?" Digby replies. It strikes him as the appropriately manly thing to say.

"Yup, I nailed the little bastard," Herker repeats. He is beside Digby now, jogging in place. Without thinking, Digby finds his feet mimicking Herker's, doing a little heel and toe action. "I told you I'd find him," Herker goes on. "Or did you think I'd forget about it after your little showstopper?"

Digby has no idea what Herker is talking about, but he decides to wait for clarification rather than ask for it. Something about the big man's pungent heavy breathing makes him feel this is a less toxic approach.

"Yup, I bet you thought I'd forgotten all about it, Maxwell," Herker goes on. "But not me. Forgive, possibly, but forget, never. You throw a beer bottle in my direction and I'll find you, one way or another."

Aha! The jettisoned beer bottle that smashed the Administration Building window. Digby shrinks away from the college president. Language-challenged as Herker may well be, his switch to the second person gives Digby the willies.

"Who was it?" Digby asks in a tone of voice that he hopes comes off as mildly disinterested.

"This'll surprise you, Maxwell," Herker says. He appears to wink, although he may just be batting away some drips of sweat with his eyelids. "Yes, I'm sure it would surprise anybody of your way of thinking."

In the moment, Digby is so curious to hear what Herker believes is his way of thinking—Digby often wonders what it is himself—that he lets the man's menacing tone pass.

"And?" Digby asks.

"It turned out to be one of those chutney farmers."

"Beg pardon?"

"Come on, Maxwell. You don't have to play that game with me. You know who I am talking about. The homos. The faggots."

It needs to be noted here that Digby is an inveterate critic of political correctness, especially when it censors colorful speech. In fact, he is of the opinion that PC-ness is one of the root causes of the decline of wit in our culture. That said, hearing Herker drop the words 'chutney farmers' and 'faggots' as if he believed they were just plain English makes Digby want to knee him in his jockstrap. Clearly, the president of the local liberal arts college is not only a racist but a homophobe. And equally as clearly, Digby needs to do something about that.

"How did you find him?" Digby asks, trying to keep his involuntary quivering to a minimum.

Herker laughs. "It wasn't that hard," he replies. "I have eyes and ears all over the campus. Loyal Louden men."

Herker's response and its shamelessly mirthful delivery remind Digby of nothing so much as the braggadocio of a Third World dictator. The man is dangerous.

"So what are you going to do—expel him?" Digby asks as neutrally as he can muster.

Herker shrugs. "I'm working on it. But you have to do these things discreetly, Maxwell. Under the radar so nobody can make a fuss about it. On the sly. It's something you get to be pretty good at in my job."

"I need to get back to work," Digby says, gesturing with his head toward Hastings Towers.

Herker lets loose with a basso guffaw the meaning of which is singularly unambiguous to Digby. The guffaw says: '*What work, Bozo? You're going to be out of a job any day now.*'

This, undoubtedly, is the source of Herker's crude candor: the college president is so certain that Digby will be gone from Louden in no time at all—just as soon as the plug is pulled on that inane magazine—that he believes he risks nothing by speaking straight from his animus. In any event, Herker's distaste for Digby Maxwell has been simmering ever since Digby's showboat, beer-bottle interception, then rose to a boil after Muffy came home from that ridiculous club of hers and went on at length about how très raffiné—*whatever the hell that means— the New Yorker was.*

But what Herker cannot imagine is that the same thought is playing in Digby's mind: his days here numbered, Digby sees nothing to lose by visiting some mischief on Miles "Kim" Herker.

Digby is suddenly a jogger himself, an exercise for his mental health. From over his shoulder he hears Herker calling after him. "Muffy says you were a big hit at her club," Herker hollers. "A real cutup."

Weeks before everything in his Louden life started to come unglued, on a late evening after a euphoric dinner with Mary, Digby had passed a couple of hours downstairs at his office desk reading *An Enquiry Concerning Human Understanding* by

David Hume, the nineteenth-century British empiricist. Digby had picked the leather-bound book at random from Bonner's bookcase after the latest issue of *Vanity Fair* had failed to hold his attention. What grabbed Digby's attention in Hume's tome was his dissection of the idea of cause and effect, particularly these lines:

"When I see, for instance, a billiard ball moving in a straight line towards another; even suppose motion in the second ball should by accident be suggested to me, as the result of their contact or impulse, may I not conceive, that a hundred different events might as well follow from the cause?"

Hume's point was that causality is all in our heads, that our minds make the connection between cause and effect based on our past experiences, say our past experiences with billiard balls. But Digby loved the idea that based on reason alone a hundred different outcomes could conceivably issue from the same cause; for example, Billiard Ball 'B' could just as likely suddenly break into a chorus of "I Wanna Hold Your Hand" after being smacked by Billiard Ball 'A.' The entire concept had the loopiness of a Road Runner cartoon. And what was most appealing about it to Digby was that from a purely *a priori* point of view, making plans and designing strategies seemed pretty much a waste of time. This fit perfectly with Digby's general belief that sometimes the best course of action is just to toss a wrench into the works and see what kind of havoc it wreaks.

Digby walks in through the front door of Hastings Towers and heads directly for June MacLane and Elliot Goldenfield's office. Both are there and surprised to see him.

"I need some advice," Digby says.

"Really?" Goldenfield intones, raising one sleek eyebrow.

"Yes. I'm afraid there's going to be some trouble on campus. Serious trouble," Digby says.

"What kind of trouble?" June asks.

Digby looks at June. There is no doubt about it, her pregnancy has radically transformed her. It must be an endocrinal thing, hormones squirting from her busy uterus to the far reaches of her body where they remove facial hair, gloss her cheeks, and smooth her formerly furrowed brow. These hormones must invade her brain too—when they arrive, do they fiddle with her philosophy? Digby somehow doubts that her 'one gender–one world' credo could hold its own against all that estrogen. All of which raises the pregnant question of just how significant can a philosophy be if a few chemical spritzes can so easily transform it?

No, that is not actually the first question that is bothering Digby's mind. That question is: who the hell is the *de facto* owner of the baby bulging from June's midriff?

Digby abruptly remembers what he is about and reaches for a wrench. "I believe your college president, Mr. Herker, is in the process of igniting a major firestorm on campus," he says. "It could get dangerous and I'm wondering if there is anything we can do about that."

Here, Digby is summoning his talent of yore, the one that once made him hot stuff in the New York magazine world: by predicting the very next thing, he is midwife to it. Nonetheless, Digby believes that at the very most all that he is doing is goosing along the inevitable.

He tells June and Elliot about Herker's so-called discovery that the bottle-thrower is a member of the campus gay group. Digby suggests—without, of course, any genuine evidence of his own—that Herker's evidence is flimsy, *way* flimsy, coming from informants in the Beer Party Republican mob. He quotes Herker's words, "faggots" and "chutney farmers," and grimaces with the pain of reiterating those words. He concludes by saying, "He has definitely crossed the line. I'm afraid a confrontation is inevitable. I hope it doesn't get out of hand."

Wrench lofted, the phone rings.

Cause and effect?

Digby sprints to his office and picks it up. "Maxwell here."

"How soon can you get over here? I've got my grandson waiting."

"Mr. Baskerton?"

"Himself."

Definitely cause and effect!

"I'll be right over."

"Wait. Maxwell, you still there? Do you have a computer? A portable computer?"

"I do."

"Bring it."

Robert Baskerton, LLB's door is wide open when Digby arrives. Baskerton is on the phone but waves him in, pointing to a seat and gesturing for him to set his MacBook on his desk.

"I've got my grandson on the phone," Baskerton says to Digby. "He wants to scoop with us." Baskerton's grandson corrects him and Baskerton says, "*Skype* with us. Do you know how to do that?"

Digby does. Baskerton hands Digby the phone and Skype data is exchanged. In a matter of minutes, Baskerton's grandson, an earnest-looking young man with stringy brown hair and rimless glasses appears on the screen. His name is also Robert, but he goes by Robbie. He is sitting on his bed in his dormitory room at M.I.T.

"Good afternoon, Mr. Maxwell," he says.

"Good to meet you," Digby replies.

"So, do you know your way around Sentry Link?"

"Nope."

"It's a personal background database. Totally legit, but pricey. Grandpa put it on his American Express card."

Baskerton smiles proudly; Digby is not sure whether that is because he is footing the bill or because he feels terribly up-to-date by dint of owning an American Express card.

"Anyhow, there aren't that many Ronald LeFevres," Robbie continues. "In fact, only one in this guy's age range. I'll UL a pic."

Digby watches Robbie do some tricky finger work on his laptop and then a photograph of Felicia Hastings' very own Ronald LeFevre pops up on Digby's screen. In the photo, however, LeFevre's hair is black and parted in the middle.

Baskerton snickers. "All that's missing is a rose in his mouth," he says.

"That your man?" Robbie asks.

"It is."

"Okay. His real name is Fredrick Linkleter," Robbie says. "Born 1952 in Wilmington, Delaware. Majored in finance and communications at Goldey-Beacom College. High honors, it says. Oh, he also goes by Nicolas Lombardi."

Baskerton snorts. "He's got a record, right?"

"Not really," Robbie says. "Nothing criminal, not even a DWI. But he's been on the losing end of a few pricey civil suits. Wait a second, okay, Gramps?"

Robbie does some more fleet computer multitasking and up on Digby's screen pops the lawsuit of one Alice Pingree Thompson versus Nicolas Lombardi, aka Fredrick Linkleter, aka Ronald LeFevre, re: obtaining funds under false pretenses. These funds amounted to in excess of two million dollars; the alleged pretense had been that Lombardi, aka Linkleter, etc., was an estate planner. Another alleged pretense was that Lombardi, aka Linkleter, etc. intended to spend the rest of his life at Ms. Thompson's side. In point of fact, he took off for Beaulieu-sur-Mer, France, as soon as said funds were deposited in his bank account. The court found in favor of the plaintiff, but the defendant ended up repaying only fifty cents on the dollar because, apparently, in merely six weeks' time he had racked up one million dollars in purchases of gifts, mostly jewelry, and all for persons other than Ms. Thompson.

Robbie then pulls up three more civil suits involving LeFevre and women of a certain age with patrician names, including one in which LeFevre actually prevailed because, as the judge wrote, "The defendant's promise of lifelong companionship and fidelity is, in the context of today's common language usage, no more binding than, in an earlier era, a wink once promised marriage." Baskerton reluctantly expresses admiration for the judge's fine turn of phrase.

And that does it. Robbie instructs Digby on how to save and print the court documents and then, after promising his grandfather to drop by during summer break, signs off.

Baskerton pours out two brandies. "Smart boy, our Robbie," he says. "What did that take—ten minutes?"

The two men clink glasses.

"To tell you the truth, I didn't expect LeFevre to be that bad. Or that obvious," Digby says.

"I did. The minute I laid eyes on him. A larcenous gigolo, head to foot."

"You must have a better eye for these things than I do," Digby says. "So, what do we do with this?"

"What do you think we do? We have a talk with Felicia Hastings."

Without a hint of forewarning, a cringe creases Digby's brow. "I'd hate to break Mrs. Hastings' heart," he says. To his surprise, he genuinely means it.

"You're talking about the woman who wants to put you and your magazine out of business, Maxwell. And by devious means."

"I guess I'm a romantic."

"I don't believe that for a minute."

"Listen, every relationship is full of *quid pro quos*. So LeFevre is a grifter, he's still giving the old girl the first good shagging of her life."

"Overrated!" snaps Baskerton. "A squirt in the dark doesn't hold a candle to a Louden sunset. Anyhow, she can do better than that chub."

"Maybe not. She's not a young woman."

"I'm an old man."

The relevance of Baskerton's status as an old man escapes Digby. The reason for his own reluctance to inform Felicia about her lover's unsavory track record also escapes him. Could his own late-in-life throbbing of the heart have altered his character so much that he is morphing into a wuss?

"Let's just think this through," Digby says. "What if we just get a hold of LeFevre alone, tell him we're wise to him, and offer him a chance to disappear quietly."

Baskerton gazes at Digby for a moment, then drinks down a slug of brandy before responding. "You're talking nonsense," he says. "You do know that, don't you, Maxwell?"

The elocutionary manner in which the lawyer delivers his question suggests that he is entertaining some serious doubts about Digby's *compos mentis*. His question is, in effect, a psychological test.

Digby has generally found it advantageous to deny that he is crazy, so he nods in agreement to Baskerton, but he cannot help himself from saying, "I just wonder if there's a delicate way to let her know."

"Jesus Christ, I'll do it myself!" Baskerton barks. He shakes his head back and forth and mutters, "A pussycat from New York—now that's a new one."

On a scale of put-downs Digby has borne, Baskerton's 'New York pussycat' rates low in both wit and weight, yet it rankles Digby all the way back to Hastings Towers, possibly because he, like many men, has always feared that truly falling in love is a severely emasculating experience. For ballast, he feels that he needs to do something masterful, if not altogether manly. In his office, he immediately dials up Clive Bosnoglian at Saatchi & Saatchi.

"Clive Bosnoglian."

"Digby Maxwell here."

"Maxwell, I was starting to give up on you."

"I've just been a little overwhelmed, doncha know?"

"Have you got those figures?" Bosnoglian asks.

"Yes. Right. Here they are. I've got ten thousand for the back page, full color. And six thousand for the insides. We could package it at fifteen."

"You've got to be kidding, Maxwell."

"Clive, I'm going to let you in on a little something that's going on here. We're already seeing our subscriptions skyrocketing. Like more than a thousand percent. Buzz is as buzz does, you know? And my people tell me these subscribers are highflyers. The hundred-and-eighty-grand-and-up bracket."

In the bathroom of Digby's upstairs suite, a pile of old copies of *Cogito* sits in a wicker basket next to the toilet. Usually, a cursory look at the table of contents is enough to relax a recalcitrant sphincter, but on occasion Digby has found himself reading an entire article. One such was titled, "Situational Ethics and Moral Relativism: The Dilemma of 'Dilemmas.'" Digby detected a rare spot of wordplay in the words following the colon, so he read on.

According to the three authors, all professors of philosophy at Dartmouth College, since the question of *a priori* first moral principles can never be resolved satisfactorily, the only problem left to the philosophy of ethics is how to apply the principles we nonetheless believe in—say the Golden Rule—to real situations. Not always easy, they say, because in real situations there can be competing claims to the same principle.

The colorful example that the professors cited was of a woman who can only obtain a lifesaving medicine for her sick husband if she sleeps with this real cad of a doctor. This woman believes in the Golden Rule; and she certainly would not want her husband to be unfaithful to her, therefore she should not sleep with the doctor. Yet she also believes that she would want her husband to do whatever was necessary to save her life if he were in the same situation. What to do, what to do.

Understandably, the article starts to get murky at this point, but Digby was relieved to see that in the end the professors opted for sleeping with the cad because "the competing principle is ultimately void in projected time"; by this they apparently meant that you cannot be unfaithful to a dead man.

What Digby took away from "The Dilemma of 'Dilemmas'" was that it was a good idea to always maintain a certain amount of moral flexibility. So, even though he had recently pledged himself to improving his character, he is certain there are valid competing reasons for laying some serious bullshit on Clive Bosnoglian. Digby cannot say exactly what these competing reasons are, but why else would he be feeling so put upon lately? (Philosophically speaking, the fact that said bullshit departs Digby's lips effortlessly is morally irrelevant.)

Bosnoglian remains silent for a count of five, then says, "I'll see if I can swing it. What's the damage for all six issues?"

"Eighty thou," Digby says. "Maybe seventy-five if we can work out a decent payment schedule."

"No problem with my client list, I gather," Bosnoglian says.

"Apple? Dewar's? Gap? We'll be honored, Clive."

"I'll have my people draw something up," Bosnoglian says. Goodbye, goodbye.

There are now more wrenches careening around in his universe than Digby can keep track of. But what is most troubling is that he has the uncomfortable suspicion that they are not wrenches at all, but boomerangs.

CHAPTER 19

Out his office window, Digby sees some ant-like busyness in the Louden College quad. From this distance, the figures also appear ant sized, but squinting Digby is just able to make out that they are wearing familiar lavender T-shirts. They scurry thither and yon; clearly, June and Elliot have set these folk afoot.

The setting sun is now slipping behind the highest dormer of the Administration Building, casting a spear-like shadow that—just for the moment—reaches all the way to the tulip beds of the Hastings Towers garden. Madeleine and Rosti's game of hide-and-seek apparently went into overtime, and June and Elliot were already gone when Digby returned from Baskerton's, so he is alone in his office. He finds himself in a John Calvin state of mind: he needs to keep busy. Either that or his disquieted brain will start to fragment. Perhaps that is why the Reformist Friar, Brother Calvin, saw work as a ticket to salvation: it kept a fella from going to pieces. Being one whole person is probably a good condition in which to be when starting out on the path to redemption.

Although laying out the heaven issue of *Cogito* is officially Madeleine's responsibility, Digby takes the task upon himself. He has no definite idea how Felicia will respond to the news that her boyfriend is a scoundrel—for all Digby knows, she may find sleeping with a cad a reasonable trade-off after forty years abed with an Aristotelian; especially considering that, as Digby recently read in Bonner's book collection, Aristotle once declared that a woman's body and sex organs were a corrupt version of a man's. But on the chance that Mrs. Hastings bows out of her relationship with LeFevre and along with him his scheme for fizzling out the magazine, Digby thinks he should be ready to go to press the moment Saatchi & Saatchi's ads come in. Even if in the stunningly unpredictable world Digby currently inhabits the idea of being prepared seems counter-intuitive at best, so does being unprepared.

Happily, Digby still knows his way around the InDesign layout software and, truth to tell, he is enjoying himself tremendously, distraction being a gratifying end in itself in spite of Kierkegaard's dictum that all distractions from one's Ultimate Fate turn one into a automaton.

Digby starts off with Rosti's epigrammatic enigma, setting it in a Christy biblical font inside a scrolled box surrounded by Tommy Gasparini's Hogarth print of St. Jerome gazing at heaven. Open with class and scholarship, then turn the page and—Bang!—an illustration from the Kacho Oji animé of *The Legend of Lost Heaven*, where Digby begins the piece about St. Peter's immigration policy in Times Roman. He pulls Chuck's first line and uses it as the headline: "Keep Them Darkies Outta Here!" Social commentary with edge and a wink. Yup, threading Tommy's graphics through the book is the way to go. It will keep the reader off-balance, alternately pondering and snickering and, above all, thinking he is sophisticated.

Digby needs to go next with his franchise player, Binx Berger, but Binx's manuscript isn't in yet so he texts his iPhone telling him that he needs it ASAP as he's their cover story— which, of course, may or may not be true—and Binx texts Digby back in real time that he'll have it for him by sunrise.

Then it's the old bait and switch, Tommy's panel from the religious comic strip, *Heavens to Betsy*, followed by what has turned out to be the issue's most substantive philosophical piece, Reverend Mary Bonavitacola's take on Paul Tillich's

'Eternal Now,' complete with some thoughtful background on from whence the idea of the eternal soul came. (The Greeks.)

Digby works his way to the last pages where, in a flash of inspiration, he sets off the MacLane & Goldenfield column (which he retitles from "In Dissent" to "Get Serious!") between two ghoulish panels from Tommy's prize find, the *Lady Death: Between Heaven and Hell* graphic novel. *Perfetto!* By God, *Cogito* now has more wry sophistication than *New York Magazine* ever had. Bring on the Jaguar account, Bosnoglian!

Other than Binx's article, the only gap remaining is Digby's piece on heaven in the cinema that he has been diddling at for weeks now. He has already requisitioned the photo stills for it—a murky, Brueghel-like heaven shot from F. W. Murnau's 1926, black-and-white masterpiece, *Faust*; a dry-ice mist heaven frame from *Here Comes Mr. Jordan*; and a garish shot of Sensory-Overload Heaven from *What Dreams May Come*. All that is missing is Digby's text. But now, pressed on by his self-imposed and arbitrary deadline, he calls his notes up onto his screen and sets to it, leading off with the immortal Monty Python line from *The Meaning of Life*—Part VII: "Do get Mr. Death a drink, dear." On it flows, effortlessly striking a delicious balance between snark and sapience.

Digby leans back in Bonner's cozy oak chair and peers again toward the dark Louden campus. No movement in the quad. He shuts down his computer, douses the lights, and lumbers upstairs to his room over the store. He pulls a Trout River from the fridge, uncaps it, and swallows a cool mouthful. By God, his little suite here feels more like home than any place he can remember.

Something flickers in the oriel window across from him. He stands and tries to take a closer gander at the flickery, but from this angle it vanishes from view, so he climbs up on his chair to try to locate it. Yup, there it is at the very far end of the campus—the president's cramped residence, if he is not mistaken. And that flicker? It appears to be a bonfire surrounded by pinpoints of arcing lights—flashlights wielded by a sizeable crowd. In a burst of athleticism that would make Kim Herker green-eyed, Digby jumps off the chair, beer bottle in hand, and heads for the phone. He is inspired to loft one last wrench into the cosmos.

He dials up the night desk of WCAX-TV in Burlington. An adolescent male voice answers.

"I'm calling from Louden," Digby says. "There's a big ruckus on campus. Burning the president in effigy."

"Obama?"

"No, Herker. President of the college. In front of his house. A mob scene. Looks menacing."

"Jesus. It's almost ten o'clock."

"I guess I called the wrong station," Digby says.

"Wait a minute. We've got a mobile unit, you know. All I have to do is call them."

"Sounds like a plan."

"But, hey, how do I know this is legit? These guys'll kill me if I pull them away from their La-Z-Boys for nothing. Like, who are you?"

"Reggie Phelps," Digby answers. "You know, from the football team. They'll remember me from the Johnson State game. I'm the one who tackled that big motherfucker in the last minute."

Fluent bullshit. As it happens, a kid named Reggie Phelps sat in front of Digby in American History at Passaic High; at the time Reggie was a superb football player. Digby feels good about keeping Reggie's name alive, wherever he is.

"I'll tell them to look for you, Reggie," the young journalist says.

Digby then offers the same exclusive story to WFFF-TV in Burlington and WNNE-TV in Windsor, before calling all the daily newspapers in a hundred mile radius—that is, both of them. He leisurely finishes off his beer, showers, combs back his mouse-colored locks, dresses collegiately in chinos and blue Oxford shirt, and heads downstairs and over to Louden Clear where he takes a stool at the bar in front of the television set. There is only one explanation for any of Digby Maxwell's actions this evening: he never matured properly.

It's quarter to twelve and there's no one in the place except Ada, the magnificent, almond-eyed bartender, and Digby. Louden Clear officially closes at midnight on Tuesdays, but Ada is allowing Digby to linger over his fourth Dewar's while she cleans up, a daunting task due to tonight's unprecedented traffic.

The heavy customer flow began at about ten-thirty when the first TV satellite truck rolled up Brigham Street, its roof-top beacon flashing. Locals, young and old, in shorts and in Talbots leisure wear, suddenly appeared, every one of them as charged up as a Louden middle schooler on a field trip to Burlington. Before heading out to the action at the Herker residence, apparently a drink was required to put it all in proper perspective. The sole Louden police car and its sur-real siren brought in the next wave, then a second TV truck brought in the next cohort of gawkers. Digby was surprised at how many folks he recognized filing in and out—the Hastings Towers weekend surveyors, Winny and her professor friends, the hyper waiter from the Moroccan restaurant, and even a bevy of Thursday Morning Club matrons, one of whom offered Digby a meaningful wink, the meaning of which escaped him. If nothing else, this wrench-toss of his was definitely providing a festive night in Louden, Vermont.

Digby makes a big show of sliding a twenty dollar bill to Ada's side of the bar, payola to let him remain in place for the local news midnight sign-off.

And finally here it is: the lead piece on WCAX-TV. A young man who appears no older than Sylvie, undoubtedly the telephone recipient of Digby's hot tip, is standing in front of Herker's cottage, the fire smoldering at a tasteful distance over his right shoulder.

"Greg van Stoot here, on location at Louden College, in Louden, Vermont," he says. He can barely contain his giddiness; Digby half expects him to blurt out, "Hi, Mom! It's *me*, Greg!"

Ada turns up the volume and leans against the bar, watching with Digby.

"A riot broke out on this campus late Tuesday night," Van Stoot continues breathlessly. "What began as a peaceful demonstration by the gay community ended with twelve arrests and one student hospitalized for cuts to his head."

"Assholes," Ada murmurs.

The boy journalist goes on to report that Louden College president, Miles Herker, had been heard referring to gay students as 'faggots' and was apparently planning to expel one of their number on unfounded charges. Digby couldn't have scripted Greg better himself.

The station now cuts to recorded images of the bonfire (alas, no effigy), students with rather lame placards reading "Herker Jerk" and "Expel *this*!", and then onscreen appears none other than the pregnant philosopher, June MacLane. Ada abruptly sets down the beer mug she has been swabbing and gazes at the television set. Some ruby redness rises on her tawny cheeks.

"This behavior by a college president is inexcusable and unacceptable," June begins, gazing urgently, yet also maternally into the camera. Here the cameraman pulls back to a two-shot of June that reveals her bulging middle. For reasons Digby does not even want to puzzle over just now, June is wearing a T-shirt bearing the legend, "Baby on Board" with an arrow pointing down toward her swollen womb.

"Bitch!" snaps Ada.

"Beg pardon?" Digby says.

"MacLane," says Ada. "She's all talk."

"And no what?"

"What do you think?" snaps Ada, bitterly.

Digby does not think, so he says nothing as he listens to June demand Herker's immediate resignation. "I am calling for a strike of all faculty and students beginning immediately. We are waiting, Mr. Herker."

Then the denouement. Just as June finishes up, the camera jerks to the front door of the president's residence where a figure has just exited and begun pacing with a regal gait toward June. It is Muffy and she is wearing a gown from some bygone era, all lace and filigree. Her hair is fastened with tortoise combs into a bun with tendrils of scarlet hair flouncing against her neck. As she pulls into the frame, she immediately makes June, by comparison, look common, a local unwed mother which, in a sense, she is. Muffy has a piece of stationery in her hand.

"I am Mildred Herker, wife of Miles Herker, and first lady of Louden College," she reads. "It is unfortunate that lies have been spoken and spread about my husband. None of it is true." Muffy now looks earnestly into the camera. "My husband is distraught. He wants everyone to know that he feels nothing but love and compassion for people of *outré* sexual orientations."

"*Outré?*" June roars.

Ada howls with laughter.

"Excuse me if I did not use *le mot juste*, Miss MacLane," Muffy says, her tone somewhere between high society-speak and pure seethe. It appears that she is going to add an explanation, perhaps pointing out that *outré* is French, her favorite *lingua franca*, but June jumps in before Muffy can go on.

"Oh, you used the right word all right," June says. "You said exactly what you meant."

"Words!" Muffy groans, grimacing.

"This is a university, Mrs. Herker. Words are our stock in trade."

Muffy is now clearly at a loss for words, so she begins marching back to her front door.

Cut back to Van Stoot. "We will have more as this story develops," he says. "Back to you, Jack, in Burlington."

It would appear that Greg van Stoot thinks he has just positioned himself for a Pulitzer. Hell, Digby would vote for him if he were on the jury. From Burlington, they are now airing a commercial for Walmart where they are running a special on snack foods. Ada clicks off the TV, then quickly scoops up the twenty, a signal that it is time for Digby to go.

"Do you still think June is a bitch?" Digby asks on his way out.

"Just to me maybe," Ada sighs. It is the unmistakable sigh of a jilted lover.

CHAPTER 20

It is only nine-thirty in the morning, but Digby is already abuzz after only five hours sleep, editing Binx Berger's just-arrived piece (like most TV writers, Binx cannot discern the difference between sketch humor and on-the-page comedic prose) in between snappy sprints up to the Louden campus to behold the aftermath of last night's high-stakes drama that is now playing out in, well, sketch humor. In less than half a day, all that appears to have sifted down from yesterday's clash of ideologies is the message that someone has called a general student strike. Indeed, what must be close to the entire Louden College student population is outside and gushing with glee. Truancy with a justification! Party time with a purpose! Never mind that none of them appears to know or care what, precisely, that purpose is. Dress is casual, high-spirited shouting mandatory, beer the fuel.

Both the college security team and the Louden police are out in force, a number of the latter decked out in helmets and ersatz acrylic face masks that make them look more like scuba divers than a SWAT team. So far, there seems to be little for them to do except to occasionally clear a pathway so that a faculty member can slip through the campus rumpus. In fact, the only sign that some kind of substantive issue has occasioned this *al fresco* wingding is Associate Professor of Gender Studies and Philosophy, June MacLane, holding forth under a willow tree with a Radio Shack PA system that amplifies the rustle of the willow branches as much as it does her voice. Digby observes that she is still wearing her "Baby on

Board" T-shirt; indeed, this touch lends her more star power and gravitas than any words she is uttering—that is, if her words were audible. At the edges of it all, a few journalists, a photographer, and the lone remaining videographer peer on, like Digby, searching warily for a flying spark that could ignite this party into a firestorm.

Back in Digby's office, Berger's piece for *Cogito* presents a more focused problem. It is written as a dialogue between St. Peter at the Pearly Gates and a TV reality show producer, Max, who is in possession of a way high concept: he wants to film contestants trying to get into heaven. In the producer's words, "It's the ultimate survival show!"

The section Digby is currently working on goes like this:

> St. Peter: We'd need to have full control over sponsors, Max.
> Max: No beer commercials, if that's what you're worried about.
> St. Peter: No, beer's not a problem—but life insurance companies, that's a definite no-no.

With, say, Bill Murray and Andy Samberg trading the lines on a fanciful set—perhaps fashioned from items borrowed from the prop room of the folks who brought us *What Dreams May Come*—and in front of a live audience with an average age of twenty-one, this is definitely boffo material. A yuk a minute. The problem, however, is that in print it reads like the repartee of two college sophomores who've had one toke too many. Actually, the only significant problem confronting Digby is whether or not he dares risk offending Binx Berger by altering his little opus. Berger is, after all, a media hotshot and with that station in life, as Digby well remembers, comes unbridled arrogance. If Digby changes a few lines of dialogue, Berger might pull his piece in a huff and that would have repercussions with *Cogito*'s sponsors—that is, if Felicia Hastings is still on board. So after hours of monkeying with Binx's prose, Digby decides instead to leave it just as it is and tweak it indirectly by composing an intro that readjusts the reader's mind-set: he writes an editor's note to the effect that the following shtick was considered too sophisticated for broadcast on national TV, but not too sophisticated for *Cogito*. No sirree, we are hipper than hip up here in philosophy-land, so hang on to your seat, lucky reader. Framing a piece is everything. And Digby is pretty sure Binx will not object to this; being deemed too sophisticated for TV is what TV writers dream about.

Digby uploads the complete interior package to the printer in Boston, cover art and ads to follow, then strolls up to the campus again where he finds Winny hanging out with the *Addison County Independent* reporter, a fifty-something Yankee with a sparkle in his eye. Winny is working her gamic magic on him and Digby mentally blesses them both.

"The muckamucks have started to arrive," Winny informs Digby.

"Who's that?"

"The Louden Board of Overseers," she replies. "Emergency session. Herker is going to explain himself."

"Is Mrs. Herker coming too? She has a way with words."

"Muffy?" Winny croons.

"*Muff-ee, elle-même,*" Digby says in heavily American-accented French, and both Winny and the Yankee chuckle with generous, insincere appreciation.

"The press is not invited to the meeting," the journalist says. "But word has it that the chairman of the board has a son who had a coming-out-of-the-closet party at the family country club. Should make things interesting."

Digby returns to his office to find Madeleine giving Rosti a neck rub as he sits in her desk chair. He looks either blissful or catatonic, it is hard to tell with the logician.

"He gets knots," Madeleine says, not missing a knead. "Listen, we received our fourteenth personal ad this morning."

"Personal as in, looking for companionship?"

"They're really pathetic," Madeleine sneers. "Shameless, actually."

Considering Madeleine's M.O. in calf-roping Rosti, Digby finds her condescension more than a little confounding, but he lets it pass. "I didn't know we carried personal ads," he says.

"We don't," Madeleine replies. "We don't even have a rate schedule for them. But that doesn't keep them from coming in."

So *Cogito*'s buzz just keeps buzzing.

"Hey, why not?" Digby says. "*The New York Review of Books* has a whole page of them. At two hundred and eighty-five bucks a hit, if memory serves. Send our companion-seekers the same rates and see who's still in. Then lay those ads out for me, will you? And ASAP—we're putting the issue to bed in three days."

"I think it's tacky," Madeleine says.

"I've always had a soft spot for the lonely," Digby says, but before Madeleine can reply the phone rings. It is Bob Baskerton. Digby takes the call in his office.

"Just had a fruitful breakfast with Mrs. Hastings," Baskerton says.

"Cantaloupe? Strawberries?" Digby feels it is in his best interest not to appear too eager.

"I hope your magazine is funnier than you are," Baskerton retorts.

"Me too," Digby says. "Did you fill Felicia in on LeFevre's background?"

"I did."

"And?"

"She took it like a soldier. No tears, no bitter remarks. Cool as a daisy in October. She didn't even ask to see my evidence."

"She trusts you."

"Yes, she does," Baskerton says, with more savor in his voice than Digby would have expected. "She even thanked me. Said it was better to hear it from me now than from someone else later."

"Well, I guess it is for the best, then. For her, I mean."

"I'm sure it is. Only part that disappoints me is the way Felicia underestimated herself—a fine woman like that."

"Could have been her marriage that did that to her. Sapped her feminine self-assurance. It's been known to happen," Digby says. As much as he would like to pursue the surprisingly personal turn their conversation has taken, he does have a more pressing question for Attorney Baskerton. "So is she okay with my new advertisers now?"

"Do you really think I would bring that up at a time like this?" he snaps.

"I guess I wasn't thinking."

"I guess not," Baskerton says, and with that he unceremoniously hangs up.

Nonetheless, Digby feels optimistic, and along with this rare sensation comes an inspiration for the cover: a gloopy still shot from *What Dreams May Come* featuring Robin Williams looking gooey-eyed at a flying dachshund in polychromatic heaven. Caption: "Paradise if you can stand it!"

Digby spends the next three hours laying out the cover, setting off the garishness of Hollywood heaven with a staid, academic-looking border—in fact, he mostly uses Bonner Hastings' old, *Reader's Digest*-like cover art, complete with a *faux* Benedict Uncial font that all but chants, "Holy, Holy, Holy." Yup, a double dose of irony before you even open the book. At the top: "Cogito / a Journal of Philosophy and Contemporary Culture" and under that, "Heaven Issue." In the upper right hand corner he features Binx Berger's name, followed by "Head Writer, *Saturday Night Live*," in über-conservative Baskerville Old Face font; but Digby colors it fuchsia, matching the wildflowers in Robin's Shangri-la. Veritable back flips of irony. Digby considers posting Chuck Jones's and Tommy Gasparini's names there too, but desists in favor of less is more. Finally, in an explosion of indefensible hubris, Digby changes the newsstand price from $7.50 to $8.95.

In wrench-throwing mode, I am a wild man.

Digby uploads the cover art to the printer's FTP site and hot steps it back to the Louden campus.

The crowd is denser now, the voices shriller, the general tenor more base. Students are herding in the direction of the Administration Building in what Digby quickly detects are two distinct groups, the same two that started it all: the gays and their earnest supporters on one side, their detractors, the all-American tea and beer partiers on the other. But this time the remainder of the student body—which is by far the great majority of the kids out here—has to vote their allegiances with their feet. With which group do they foot? This is what the pedagogues typically call a 'unique teaching moment.' And this time the pedagogues are absolutely right: this is undoubtedly the defining moment of each student's four years at Louden College, one that may very well inform the rest of his or her life: when forced to decide, on what principle do they ultimately stand? Whether or not this teaching moment is worth two hundred thousand dollars of their parents' money is an altogether different question.

"It's show time!" Winny calls to Digby from the back of the gay rights group.

Digby saunters up alongside her, noting that she and the Yankee journalist are now holding hands. God love them, they seem perched between 'We shall overcome' camaraderie and gladsome carnality.

"Wassup?" Digby asks.

"Press conference. Out on the Administration Building terrace," Winny replies.

"Where it all began," Digby says. "Site of the blind-flying beer bottle. Who are the featured speakers?"

"The chairman of the board and Herker himself for starters. But there's some scuttlebutt that June MacLane will have her turn too. Somebody saw her run back to her room to change her clothes."

"I hope she doesn't dispense with her "Baby on Board" T-shirt. I think it has serious cross-over appeal," Digby says.

"Her ace in the hole, so to speak," says the Yankee with Yankee drollery. Yup, Digby fully endorses the wry gent's candidacy as Winny's bedmate.

The two packs of students are nearly equal in number, and as they crowd abreast one another at the perimeter of the terrace—where the police have erected a barrier constructed out of what must be the only materials available to them: yellow plastic ribbon inscribed with the words, CRIME SCENE—some jostling erupts. Also some ugly utterances, like "pansy lover!" and "shit for brains!" A teaching moment this may be, but it would be absurd to believe it would instantly instill these kids with wit.

Digby now sees Kim and Muffy Herker through the long windows of the Administration Building parlor, an unusually handsome, blond-haired, six-and-a-half-footer between them. All three appear dressed for some kind of blue blood gala, at once sporty and stylish. Digby is particularly struck by the pink silk handkerchief sprouting from Kim's blazer breast pocket; it looks a bit *poofy*—an excellent touch. Digby wonders if Herker consulted a public relations expert. Kim's brow is furrowed as he studies a piece of paper in his hands, undoubtedly his press conference script. For his sake, Digby hopes Kim's wife did not pen it for him. And, yes indeed, a few feet to one side of them, is June. She is wearing a shiny maternity dress of the same pink hue as Herker's hanky.

"Hi there."

Digby turns around. It is Mary. She smiles and comes up beside him. He feels his heart do back flips far more poignant than back flips of irony could ever be.

"I'm praying for a happy ending," he says to her over the din.

"Scratch a cynic," she replies. From the gleam in her eyes, Digby senses that she approves of his sentiment and he senses a fleeting stab of self-reproach—at the very least, his wrench-throwing was responsible for hastening this grand denouement.

But hold on, there is more to this denouement than Digby, once the supreme spotter of the very next thing, foresaw—indeed, more than he could have foreseen in his wildest forecasts: Mary kisses his cheek. No routine peck, this—it is a genuine smacker.

Digby smiles blissfully at her just as the devilishly good-looking six-and-a-half-footer he spotted through the window steps out onto the terrace. The man nods formally to the assembly, then brushes back a lock of his blondness that has flopped onto his forehead. Digby gathers that he is the father of the allegedly gay young country clubber; if his son has even a fraction of his father's good looks, he must be a much sought after gay blade.

"I am Daryl Aylesworth, Chairman of the Board of Overseers of Louden College," he begins. "And what we all have been presented with today is a unique teaching moment."

Digby grimaces, as they say, inwardly. Mary has taken his hand and now squeezes it.

What exactly is going on here with this digital intimacy? Is it merely Unitarian fellowship? Is she qualifying her foot vote for gay rights with a hand vote for her own heterosexuality? But what about that squeeze, huh?

Does Mary—please, God!—actually like me? Like me a whole lot after all?

After a series of sleep-inducing platitudes about the virtue of reaching for a consensus, Chairman Aylesworth abruptly executes an unexpected change of field and starts talking about his days at Louden as captain of its football team, president of his fraternity, and secretary of the Young Republicans. These were happy days, he says. He fit right in, he felt good about himself. He met his wife while here at Louden. He made lifelong friends here too. Then, without any modulation of his voice, Aylesworth says, "In fact, it wasn't until many years later that I realized what an asshole I had been."

A frozen moment while the word 'asshole' hovers, hummingbird-like, on the edges of the assembled crania, then a roll of gasps and giggles as it penetrates one cerebral lobe after another. These gasps and giggles appear to be distributed equally among the warring packs. Winny, the Yankee, Mary, and Digby are among the gaspers.

"I had an easygoing contempt for Jews, blacks, liberals, anybody who took their courses seriously, ugly people and, of course, homosexuals. *Especially* homosexuals," Aylesworth goes on.

Digby admires his tone as much as his message. No saccharine sincerity, no *mea culpa* histrionics, not even a hint that he is conscious of the fact that he is venturing outside the bounds of common Louden discourse. No, Aylesworth's tone is as matter-of-fact as a sports announcer reporting a play-by-play.

"I never gave a thought to it—my contempt," he continues. "I knew every joke and snide remark about these so-called contemptible types as well as I knew my scrimmage playbook. Knew them by heart. Recited them automatically. I learned this contempt without thinking about it for a minute, but that's not the important part. Because I'll tell you what I did know—I did know my jokes and quips hurt these people. Hurt them even if they didn't hear my saying them. Hurt them because of the climate it set here at Louden. And I didn't give a rat's ass about that."

Aylesworth pauses here, a cloud of funk unexpectedly settling on his fine brow as if he has just tuned in to his own words, but it passes as quickly as it arrived.

"I want to apologize for that, all of it," the chairman says quietly. "I am very sorry. Sorry for who I was then and what it meant to many others here at Louden. I hope we can start doing something different here today. Thank you."

Mary and Digby do a mutual super-hand squeeze. Its meaning is unambiguous: they are both moved by Aylesworth. Being genuinely moved at the same time and in the same place—being moved together—promotes a species of intimacy that is unfamiliar to Digby at this late date in his career. It is, he realizes, a supreme form of intimacy.

Aylesworth gestures through the window and now President Herker comes slowly walking out onto the terrace followed at a discreet few feet by his first lady. He is displaying what Digby's mother used to call 'a brave face,' which is to say he looks defeated. Digby believes that he is now going to publicly tender his resignation—for the good of dear old Louden. But before Herker reaches center stage, a barrage of 'boos' bursts from the gay contingent. The opposing tribe instantly answers back with a chant that Digby suspects was pre-orchestrated, "Herker must stay! Homos must go!" Digby has to admit that distasteful as this chant is, it is kind of catchy. It is also the long-anticipated spark.

A young man sporting a lavender T-shirt belts a chanting young man wearing a "Louden Varsity Squash" T-shirt right in the larynx. Then a pony-tailed blonde on the opposite side of the divide knees a pony-tailed brunette on the gay side. Screams, yelps, and, in a trice, general combat is engaged.

Winny and her friend sprint off, out of harm's way, but neither Mary nor Digby seem to be able to move, even if they both believe it would be the prudent thing to do. Instead, they stand perfectly still, their arms wrapped around one another, their heads tucked down, cheek to cheek.

Police whistles pierce the clamor. Then, out of the corner of one eye, Digby sees the uniforms come rushing into the melee, batons raised. A loud whack, then another. It is terrifying.

"Please! Please! For the love of God, please!"

This cry, in a deep baritone, seems to come from the heavens. For starters, it has the resonance and authority of a deity, perhaps a Greek god, say Prometheus. But more to the point, it very much does appear to come down at them from overhead. Outdoor Yamaha speakers? Somebody on the roof of the Administration Building? Virtually everyone present, including the police, suspend their fists and batons to gaze upward.

And there they behold Miles "Kim" Herker riding astride the broad, square shoulders of Daryl Aylesworth. The vertical duo is charging into the center of the warring tribes, their combined height easily ten feet. They look glorious, astounding, and even vaguely mythological—a double-blazered Chiron.

"Please!" Herker cries again. "We are better than this!"

His voice has the timbre of a Shakespearian actor. It has power and commanding urgency. To be sure, there is something wildly comical about two middle-aged men in coats and ties doing the piggyback thing, but this act also vouches for sublime courage, daring imagination, and the spot-on reflexes of born athletes. Further, it strikes Digby that Herker's legs slung over Ayesworth's shoulders, crotch to neck, has vaguely homoerotic overtones.

In any event, it works. Arms are dropped to sides, heads are bent in embarrassment. A brief, stunned silence.

"Thank you," Herker says, still astride his mount. "We have all made mistakes here. I certainly know I have. I deeply regret them. But I am not too old or too stubborn to change. And I want to thank the board of overseers and Mr. Aylesworth in particular." Here—swear to God—he pats Aylesworth, his faithful steed, on the top of his golden head. "Because they have given me another chance, a chance to make things right."

A number of the gay contingent again starts to raise their voices in protest that apparently he is not resigning after all, but Herker soldiers on. "As a start in that direction, I am appointing June MacLane as Associate Dean of Students with a full vote on the student policy committee of Louden College. Effective immediately. Miss MacLane? Come on out here."

June, head high and stately, steps onto the terrace arm-in-arm with none other than Ada, the blushing barmaid. For the occasion, Ada has donned a teal, Vera Wang knock-off halter dress. She looks gorgeous in the extreme. Indeed, the men in both camps cannot take their eyes off her. Many of the women in both camps also.

"A miracle," Mary whispers to Digby.

"Of nature?" Digby asks.

Mary laughs. "That too," she says. "But the whole image. And what it means."

"What *does* it mean?" Digby asks, but before Mary can reply June begins to speak.

"President Herker, I am honored. And I accept. Together we will create a more tolerant, happier Louden College. One where people can proudly be themselves without shame or fear."

Then it is June's turn to pile on with bromides about broadmindedness and respecting differences, demonstrating once again that those on the fringe can be just as banal as those in the mainstream. Mary takes this opportunity to pick up her whispered conversation with Digby.

"June called me about an hour ago," she says. "Wanted me to be her onstage consort. But I declined. Said it would send a confusing message. I told her to find a sister lesbian for the occasion in order to demonstrate her pride. She sounded hurt, but I thought she sounded relieved too. She and Ada were a hot item before she became pregnant. Look at them! Delicious, huh?"

"Delectable," Digby replies.

June appears to be winding down. Herker dismounts and, apparently following June's lead, hooks up with his Muffy and the pair mosey up beside June and Ada, Daryl Aylesworth shuffling behind them. Daryl is slightly stooped, his back a little the worse for wearing Herker. The five of them line up side-by-side and smile out upon the assembly.

The entire tableaux has a corny, photo-op-at-the-conclusion-of-a-Mid-East-peace-conference gloss to it, but that is clearly just the ticket. All traces of belligerence have evaporated from the erstwhile combatants beyond the CRIME SCENE barrier. Camera clicks fill the air. Digby's eyes are now drawn to Muffy Herker's face. She, alone, appears discontented up there, her mouth drawn tight, her heavily mascaraed eyes narrowed. Does this merely come from wounded vanity at having to share the spotlight—and share it with the magnificent Ada, no less? Or is some deeper resentment at play on her brow?

Muffy provides the answer forthwith. She pivots toward her husband, reaches both hands around his neck, and yanks his head down level with hers, face to face, whereupon she plants a long, steamy smooch on his lips. Digby is certain that this act is not born of a sudden passion for her hubby. No, Muffy Herker, with her gift for dramatic expression, is definitely making a public pronouncement, to wit: *Yes, but* Sacré bleu, *we all still know that the man-woman thing is the* real *thing!*

Ada and June read Muffy's meaning instantly. So they do exactly what the situation demands: they wrap their arms around one another and produce an even longer, even more succulent kiss complete with some visible, slinky tongue work. What the onlookers have before them is a kissing contest the likes of which have never been seen at any state fair.

Digby surveys the mob of Herker supporters, the *über-*loyal Louden men and women. Have they tuned in to the high political stakes involved in this smooch competition? Will they, too, be inspired to reassert the natural supremacy of heterosexuality—perhaps with some more chants or even a few renewed pokes and punches?

Nope. And the reason for this has nothing at all to do with anyone's pride in his or her sexual orientation. No, the men and even many of the women in both groups are way too turned on by the sight of the scrumptious Ada getting lusty in her spaghetti-strapped halter dress to have a single thought about ideology. Hell, she could be making out with a rock for all they care. A lusty young beauty of either orientation whips identity politics every time.

Muffy has lost the contest big-time, knows it, and promptly leads President Herker by the hand back into the Administration Building. Aylesworth follows, then June and Ada—but not before they perform a quick, giggly reprise of their frenchie. It elicits cheers from one and all.

"Perfect," Mary says. "Every last bit of it."

Digby is pretty sure he knows what she means. June, with her new job and status, not to mention a gorgeous woman with whom she seems poised to again share her bed, will undoubtedly be less preoccupied with parenthood, especially shared parenthood with a straight woman. Like all good wrench throws, this one appears to have had some marvelous, totally unpredictable consequences.

Mary and Digby are now sitting on what he likes to think of as their personal rock near the woods on the outskirts of Louden. They are still holding hands, glory be. Winding back from the Administration Building terrace, they had some fun creating an imaginary highlights reel of the athletic press conference, finally deciding that the June–Ada kiss trumped the Herker–Aylesworth piggyback ride, astonishing as that was, for the opening sequence. They have also had some intermittent hand squeezes, the meaning of which Digby dares not contemplate. They sit quietly for a long while, then Mary says, "That talk we had the other night. Out here. It helped more than you can imagine."

"I'm glad," Digby says.

"Cathartic, I guess. And clarifying."

"Good," Digby says.

"I'm giving up my pulpit," Mary goes on. "After the baby is born. It's a boy, by the way. Reuben. I'm naming him Reuben."

The patronymic version of the continuum hypothesis.

"Sounds right," Digby says. "What will you do?"

"Teach," Mary says. "I found a job teaching high school in Rockport. Rockport, Massachusetts. That's where I'm from."

Digby does a mental Mapquest—Rockport is only a three-hour drive from Louden. This is good.

"I had almost made up my mind before all this happened today," Mary goes on. "But now I am convinced that it will be easier, much easier than I was afraid it would be. You know, June will be more okay with it."

"I'm sure she will," Digby says.

A long stillness. Then, for the first time, Digby is the one to plant a kiss—on Mary's sweet lips. It is divine.

"I'll visit you," he says.

"I certainly hope so," she says.

CHAPTER 21

Toward the end of her life, Digby's mother developed a postscript to her theory of Unremitting Universal Decay and she named this P.S. 'Salvation' in heavy, ironic quotation marks. She was a Catholic, of course, but Cynthia-Marie Maxwell's notion of salvation was far more interesting and fanciful than, say, St. Augustine's. She saw salvation more as a trick ending than as a reward for good works or deathbed conversions. On the philosophical spectrum of teleological outcomes, Mrs. Maxwell's occupied the space assigned to 'goofy blessings.'

All of this clearly made an indelible impression on Digby's own worldview. He, too, has a thing for quirky finales, but in his metaphysics the name for it is luck. Good luck. *His.* No matter how much he fucks things up—and clearly fucking things up is the *leitmotif* of his life—he remains optimistic about a lucky, if tricky, ending.

Indeed, even Digby's mother would have concluded that 'The Kiss,' as Digby would ever after designate it, was none other than her son's Salvation, the beginning of his happy ending, his long-awaited goofy blessing.

Possibly.

Digby is sitting at his office desk with the page proofs of the *Cogito* Heaven Issue in his hands. The FedEx man just delivered them along with a package from babyGap containing a pair of blue, fleece-lined dinosaur booties for Reuben

Jr. who, as of June's latest checkup, is due in fourteen days. The proofs look splendid—wry, classy, brimming with visual wit—and Digby is pleased, although not as pleased as one might expect, just as he had merely smiled when Bob Baskerton phoned him with the news that Mrs. Hastings had officially reversed course and given her approval of the Saatchi & Saatchi ads. Digby just cannot summon up the old self-congratulatory spirit that used to come so easily to him.

What he would mostly like to do right now is to show the proofs to Mary, especially the spectacular way her piece on 'The Eternal Now' jumps off the page next to the *Heavens to Betsy* panel of St. Peter who, in the illustrator's imagination, resembles a bearded Mr. Magoo. But Mary is once again in Rockport furnishing her new digs and meeting with her prospective colleagues at Rockport High and interviewing nannies. In the weeks since The Kiss, Digby and Mary have spent time together only twice, both delightful, but both kissless. Digby has to admit to himself that he is a bit jealous of Mary's excitement about her new life. He also has to admit to himself that it is just plain silly to feel jealous about that. At least, he hopes that it is just plain silly.

Digby decides that his next best option is to immediately call a meeting of his staff and show them the product of their hard work. It is a team spirit-building tactic that he learned from Phil Winston, who undoubtedly learned it while trading management tips in the Yale Club common room. Digby reaches both June and Elliot on their cell phones, but is unable to contact Rostislav at his only phone, a landline in his department office that is without an answering machine; so he saunters out to Madeleine's desk where she is industriously plugging in personal ads submitted at the eleventh hour. These now occupy two pages of the renovated *Cogito*.

"We're having a staff meeting at three," Digby tells Madeleine. "Kind of a celebration for our first issue—my first issue, that is."

Madeleine nods, but continues typing.

"I wasn't able to reach Rosti though," Digby goes on. "Can you—you know—*position* him?"

"Rosti is no longer with us," Madeleine replies.

"He's what?"

"He's on his way back to the Institute. In Moscow. He may even be there by now."

Although Madeleine has delivered this information in a dispassionate voice, Digby naturally suspects her tone to be a cover-up for a broken heart.

"I'm sorry to hear that," he says.

"I'm not."

"Really? I thought you and he were—"

"We were," Madeleine says, finally looking up at Digby with what appears to be a world-weary expression on her heretofore unsophisticated face. "It's over. I had to put the kibosh on it. That's why he left."

So, it was the logical positivist whose heart was crushed! Digby finds this news more disheartening than he would have thought it merited. Because, just below Digby's consciousness, this news stabs at his increasingly anxious faith in the constancy of the female heart.

"Ran its course, eh?" he says, trying to balance nonchalance with intimate concern.

Madeleine shrugs. "If you really want to know, he just got to be too much. Too heavy. He wanted to get married, for God's sake. Get married and stay here in Louden forever and ever."

"But, uh, that's not what you had in mind?" Digby ventures.

"Of course not. I mean the whole idea was he was only here for one term. A one-termer, you know?"

"I see," Digby says, starting back to his office before Madeleine can see the shock of middlebrow disapproval that is contorting his facial features. He is now quite sure that love has not merely weakened him, it has transformed him into a bourgeois saphead.

Again taking a cue from Phil Winston's playbook, Digby decides to make the staff meeting festive by ordering in some snack food. He looks through the Louden Yellow Pages for a pizza joint that delivers. He finds three and deliberates on his choices for a few moments; he sees it as an executive decision. He settles on Mario's Oven and is about to dial when the phone rings. Madeleine answers it, then calls to him, "It's for you."

Digby picks up. "Maxwell here," he says, still in executive mode.

"Hi, it's Felicia." Mrs. Hastings sounds positively girlish.

Mrs. Hastings and Digby have not spoken a word to one another since the dressing down she gave him in her parlor over what she referred to as the 'obscene' ads that Saatchi & Saatchi had proposed. Digby has heard that Ronald LeFevre left Louden literally under the cover of night on the very day of Felicia's fateful breakfast meeting with Bob Baskerton. That was only two weeks ago, but by tone of voice, she sounds as if she has recovered completely from both shock and heartbreak, not to mention remorse and embarrassment for having behaved so deplorably under LeFevre's tutelage.

"Nice to hear your voice, Felicia," Digby says, feeling giddily absolvitory.

"I hear you're having a special staff meeting this afternoon," she says cheerfully.

Whatever else may have changed, clearly *sub-rosa* campus communications have not slowed any.

"Yes. A little bit of a celebration," Digby says. "Show off the page proofs of the new issue."

"So I hear. Mind if I join the fun?"

"I'd be honored," Digby says.

Even before he bids goodbye to Felicia, Digby realizes that pizza simply will not do and, still in the spirit of inclusion, he phones Winny to see what she can cook up on such short notice.

"I have a half a box of spanakopita in the freezer," Winny says. "And I can whip up some tzatziki. Maybe pick up one of those raw veggie trays at the Grand Union. It'll be Greek themed. In honor of Aristotle or whoever."

"You're a doll, Winny."

"Now you tell me."

"By the way, how goes it with that dashing reporter from the *Addison County Independent*?"

"Oh, him? Kaput. E.D. problems."

It takes Digby a moment to decode these initials: 'Erectile Dysfunction,' the drug industry's snappy euphemism for what used to be called impotence. Under its former name, it was a shameful condition, whether occasional or permanent, but now that it can be addressed by a pill, E.D. is clearly the subject of casual conversation, like discussing someone's athlete's foot or asthma. Digby briefly considers suggesting Cialis for the poor bloke, but decides to skip it. Digby also briefly notes that this is the second perfunctory rejection of a male suitor that he has heard about today, but he decides to skip that thought too.

At the last minute, Digby dashes out to what is known in Vermont as a package store and picks up a magnum of California Champagne although, as the earnest young clerk explains, it is not legitimately Champagne because it was not made with grapes from the Champagne region. (Feeling cute, Digby inquires in what state the Champagne region is located.)

Soon after Digby returns, Winifred arrives with enough food for a church social. She also has brought along her portable microwave oven to serve up the spanakopita warm and creamy.

June MacLane is the first guest to arrive, at three o'clock on the button. She is merry and bloomy. She immediately asks for a peek at the proofs and Digby hands them over apprehensively, but June bursts out laughing the minute she scans the cover art with its nutty still shot from *What Dreams May Come*. Indeed, it appears as if June has not had a negative thought in quite some time; and Digby's guess is that this has more to do with her new deanship and her renewed relationship with

Ada than it does with her most notable feature, her Reuben Jr.-filled belly. No "Baby on Board" T-shirt for June today—rather a stylish, red tunic with a scoop neck, revealing the curvy top of her newly expanded bosom. Digby's sole interest while eyeing this anatomical feature is atypical for him—indeed, atypical for most men—he only wonders about function and utility, to wit, whether June is going to breast-feed little Reuben. He certainly hopes not.

"I think it's a hoot," June announces after finishing her perusal of the proofs.

"Terrific," says Digby. Perhaps Elliot Goldenfield will end up having to write future dissent columns on his own.

"When I told Ada I was going to see the heaven proofs, she said, 'Oh, really? How did they prove it?' " June says, smiling with a paramour's pride.

No lover's rejection there, thank God.

Elliot Goldenfield walks in on June's line, raises one eyebrow sardonically, grabs a carrot, dips it in the bowl of tzatziki, and sits down on one of the settees without uttering a word. He does not ask to see the proofs and Digby certainly does not feel like proffering them. Then the final guests arrive, walking in single file into Digby's office, Felicia, Madeleine, and—*who is this?*—none other than Counselor Baskerton. This occasions a flurry of cheek pecks and hugs, plus some warm pats of Reuben Jr.'s vessel.

The sole exception to this greeting frenzy is, unsurprisingly, Elliot, who remains seated and munching. Digby notices that Elliot does, however, keep shooting inquisitive glances at Felicia Hastings, and it does not take Digby long to divine their meaning: Elliot is wondering if his moment has finally arrived; if Felicia, brought back to her senses, will now do the right thing and return to her late husband's fondest wishes, namely to name Elliot Goldenfield editor-in-chief of *Cogito* magazine so that the journal can resume Bonner Hastings' mission of sober scholarship. In truth, Digby had not seriously entertained that possibility until just this minute, and in this minute it does not seem like a farfetched eventuality at all. Appointing Digby to the job had been part of LeFevre's grandly schemed con game, but with LeFevre gone, why shouldn't Digby—aka The Patsy, The Gull, The Chump—be gone too? Digby experiences a throb of insecurity, not his first of the day; they seem to have been coming at him from oblique angles all day now. He is, however, somewhat relieved to observe that Felicia does not answer Elliot's glances with any of her own.

Digby feels the need to assert some authority—not too much or too obviously—but he believes he should at least make a gesture that suggests he is still top man at *Cogito*. He dashes upstairs, withdraws the bottle of faux Champagne from his kitchen fridge, and brings it back to his office party. To Digby's relief, Baskerton offers to pop the cork, a task that has always reminded Digby all too vividly of his terrifying, short-lived career as a football place-kick holder.

Plastic cups poured, Digby proposes a toast to *Cogito* and its hard-working staff, to the late Bonner Hastings and his courageous vision, to Bonner's intelligent and warmhearted widow, and finally, for no reason that he can determine, to Rostislav Demidov, whose devotion to *a priori* truth has inspired them all. Digby intones this last bit as if he were delivering a eulogy, and everyone present, even Goldenfield, appear appropriately touched. That is when Felicia Hastings takes a short, aristocratic stroll to her late husband's oak desk chair, seats herself, planting her Champagne glass on the desk, and says, "So, what do we have in mind for the next issue?"

Everyone immediately take seats around her. Baskerton brings Madeleine's desk chair to just inside the doorway and sits there. Digby, his accustomed chair taken, is left to setting himself down on the settee next to Goldenfield.

"The philosophy of love," Digby finally replies, his voice less steady than should be that of a man who is attempting to assert his authority.

"And sex," chimes in Madeleine.

Felicia smiles and nods with a display of grace that makes Digby think of a Queen granting a reprieve of execution to a rogue who has just given the right answer to a tricky riddle put to him as his last chance for salvation.

By God, I still have my job!

"This is just off the top of my head," offers June. "But what about a piece about Sappho's love life? She apparently had a wild old time with Aphrodite on a visit to Olympus."

Before Digby can even think of a suitable response, he sees Felicia look over at Baskerton. A silent, lightning fast communication passes between them, and again Felicia gives with the regal nod.

Or do I still have my job?

This show is running, but not by Digby. Not by Elliot either, but that is small consolation. Felicia and her attorney are clearly in charge here. Digby has not a clue about what's up, but he is now convinced this Queen has as many lives as Cleopatra.

Elliot raises his hand and says, "I'm thinking of something from Nietzsche, the concept of *über*-love. The form of superior love between superior beings."

Again, there is a flash consult between Felicia and Baskerton, this time observed by everyone in the room who now look to her for her reaction. No regal nod comes forth. In spite of himself, Digby is pleased that Elliot has struck out, but there now seems little doubt that although Digby may still be the editor in name, the editor is now the Queen's pawn. Digby experiences a brief rush of nostalgia for the good old days when LeFevre was calling the shots. At least LeFevre left Digby to his own devices while he was tying a noose around his neck.

"Let's take a week or two to think about ideas," Felicia says. "Then we can have a lively discussion at our next meeting."

With perfect timing, Winny enters the office carrying a tray of piping hot spanakopita and goes directly to Felicia, offering her first dibs. Felicia chooses and bites. Digby takes this opportunity to present Felicia with the *Cogito* proofs. Baskerton rises and now stands behind her as she leafs through the pages. In a matter of seconds, they are both chuckling. All is looking good in Digby's Heaven Issue.

Now June rises and says she is sorry that she has to leave such a lovely party, but she has to attend a meeting of the newly inaugurated 'Questioning' Club. 'Questioning' is the 'Q' now appended to LGBT—Lesbian/Gay/Bisexual/Transgendered—and it applies to people questioning their sexual identity. Digby finds this 'Q' puzzling; it puts him in mind of the Red Hot Chili Pepper lyric, "If you have to ask/You'll never know/Funky motherfucker."

"I'm sworn to secrecy," June says gaily at the door. "But one of our new members comes to meetings in a varsity football shirt!"

A few minutes later Goldenfield leaves glumly, mumbling something that no one hears, Madeleine returns to her office and the personal ads, and then Mrs. Hastings rises and, joined by Baskerton, starts for the door.

"This was delightful, Maxwell," she says, offering her hand. For a moment, Digby thinks he is being asked to kiss that hand, possibly on bended knee, but Felicia, sensing his awkwardness, now pats his shoulder with said hand. "Well done," she says.

Baskerton follows with another shoulder pat and then, with a nod and an air kiss, they are gone.

"Well, I thought that went well," says Winny.

"I'm not so sure," Digby replies, busying himself by gathering up the plastic glasses.

"I wouldn't bother about Felicia's taking-charge act," Winny says. "She just needed to get her mojo back. It was a dignity thing. Not to worry, Digby."

It was only then that Digby noticed that Felicia and Basker-ton had taken the page proofs with them.

"What are you doing here, Digby?" Mary asks, getting out of her car in front of the Unitarian Church. It is just past eight in the evening.

"Loitering," Digby says.

"With intent?" Mary laughs.

"You don't know the half of my intent," Digby replies. It is meant as a witticism, but even as he utters these words he can hear their doloroso overtones. "Need any help with anything?"

"I'm good," she says, holding up a canvas bag, apparently the only luggage for her two-day round trip to Rockport.

"So, have you eaten?" Digby asks.

Jesus, if I sounded any needier she would hook me up to a leash and bring me to the Humane Society.

"Actually, I—well, sure, I can always eat something," Mary says.

"Couscous?"

"Sure."

'Sure'? Not 'yes-yes'? The magic is definitely gone.

Their conversation at the Moroccan's is lively and warm, consisting mostly of Mary's droll review of her nanny appli-cants, one of whom she guiltily rejected solely because she was the spitting image of Esme Cullen in the Twilight films. Digby tells her about the page proof party, making it sound more hilarious and far less disquieting than it actually was. They exchange plenty of happy looks, but no hands are extended across the table, not a single digit touches, not even a glancing brush of skin.

On their way back to the church, after a thirty-plus year absence, the devil once again abruptly takes up residence inside Digby and he instructs him thusly, "Either you kiss this woman now or I will set you on fire," or words to that effect. Digby tries to reason with him, but his arguments fall flat, not only to the devil, but to himself. Mary has been chatting animatedly about the wooden cradle she purchased for Reuben Jr. and, as they approach the church door, she is describing the hand-carved infinity symbol at the head of said cradle. This is when Digby, lips puckered and aimed, executes the devil's bidding.

Mary does not turn away, offering cheek in lieu of lips, but she might as well have. This kiss lacks resonance. In fact, to Digby it feels as responsive as smooching a lamb kabob. Satanic immolation would have been preferable.

"I'm sorry, Digby," Mary says. "I've got so much on my mind these days."

The devil is not forthcoming with any possible responses to this. Digby simply gazes at Mary looking far more forlorn than any self-respecting man in his forties should.

"Please try to understand," Mary says, then after a moment adds, "Hey, you're my friend who doesn't take everything so damned seriously, remember? I count on you for that. You're the yang to my yin. My perspective." With that, she gives Digby a quick hug and disappears inside the Universalist Unitarian Church of Louden.

On his way home to Hastings Towers—betwixt parsing and reparsing every word Mary said, dwelling obsessively on her use of the word 'friend'—Digby breaks into a bitter laugh. He has just remembered that in the back of his mind was the idea to ask Mary to join him on his trip to California for his daughter's wedding.

Ha, ha.

"De Beauvoir notes that women may view physical love as a debasement of their feelings of self-worth and dignity, thus many resort to frigidity, while others will give in to their carnal instincts only after being reassured of their lover's love for them. Yet, as De Beauvoir writes, 'in giving her pleasure, the man *increases* her attachment—*he does not liberate her.*'"

Digby is reading his third consecutive critique of Simone de Beauvoir's essay, "The Woman in Love," in a window seat somewhere over Buffalo. De Beauvoir, considered by many the mother of modern feminist philosophy, apparently had affairs with fellow existentialist, Jean-Paul Sartre, he who frowned upon turning oneself into an 'object,' and with Nelson Algren, he who frowned upon sleeping with anyone in possession of troubles worse than one's own. Simone also indulged in some *à trois* action with J-P and various Parisian cuties. Quoth Jean-Paul to Simone early in their relationship, "What we have is an *essential* love; but it is a good idea for us also to experience *contingent* love affairs."

These are philosophers? To Digby, Sartre's line sounds like a scumbag justifying his pigatude with some existential bafflegab.

Digby's in-flight library was assembled to coach him in the key concepts of the philosophy of love and sex so that he will be able to say something moderately knowledgeable at the upcoming staff meeting of *Cogito*. This seems like a particularly good idea because Felicia Hastings will be in attendance, and it may have inadvertently slipped her mind that in large part she originally chose Digby to be editor on the basis of his stunning ignorance of philosophy. But during Digby's final California wedding pack-up, when he found that there was only room for so many books in his carryon, his selection narrowed down to philosophical texts on women's love—or often, lack thereof—for men. Digby's need for education on this subject is only partially job-related.

The essays and reviews that Digby has read so far—most of them hybrids of moral philosophy and depth psychology—are gloomy bordering on grim. If the writers were not decrying the way men objectify women, they were crowing that the entire male enterprise is juvenile, dumb, and doomed to extinction. And in one article in *Hypatia: The Journal of Feminist Philosophy*, a learned professor pointed out that statistically women are more sexually excited by men who treat them roughly than by men who treat them with respect, so for the majority of women the concepts of love and sex are "distantly related at best." Digby had to stop reading the article soon after that 'distantly related' part. After a few minutes of heartfelt dread, he finally calmed himself by observing that *Hypatia* had even fewer ads than the old *Cogito*.

Mary is on Digby's mind. Relentlessly. The soundtrack for these thoughts is taken in its entirety from his father's *Magic of Love* boxed set, most often from Nat King Cole's rendition of "When I Fall in Love"—"When I fall in love, it will be forever/Or I'll never fall in love." Aristotle's Law of the Excluded Middle in song.

Digby is met at the door of his room at the Creekside Inn in Palo Alto by none other than the former Phil Winston and his wife, Digby's former wife, Mrs. Fanny Weinstein. Someone, possibly the statistically minded groom, has assigned rooms by kinship connections, so Phil and Fanny have chambers across from Digby's and they happen to be exiting theirs as he is about to enter his.

"What a *mitzvah!*" Phil says, pumping Digby's hand. Apparently along with his new old name, Phil has replaced his hipster-speak with Long Island Yiddish.

"A *mitzvah* that certainly raises the bar," Digby responds, hoping there is a Jewish joke hidden somewhere in his rejoinder. He has his magnetic key card in his other hand and is turning it about trying to figure which end is up.

"Hello, Digby," Fanny says with considerably less enthusiasm than her current husband evinced.

"Hi," Digby says brightly. "Congratulations!"

"We got them to break the glass," Phil says.

"Beg your pardon?"

"The wineglass," Phil says. "At the end of the service. Just as a gesture, you know. A recognition."

Considering that Sylvia, if anything, is half-Episcopalian and half-Catholic and that Ahmed is Muslim, Digby is not sure who is being recognized or why, although, come to think of it, it does seem likely that the gestured-to is the man who is footing the wedding bill.

At the prenuptials dinner on the Creekside patio, Digby is seated next to the groom's father, Dil Shad, a handsome fellow in his sixties with a full head of silky white hair. Not only does Dil Shad already know Digby's name, but where he went to college and his current position as editor of a philosophy magazine in Vermont. Digby cannot help but wonder if Dil sprang for two hundred bucks to run his name through Sentry Link.

"In Tehran, in-laws traditionally fight with each other," Dil Shad says, smiling as he fills Digby's wineglass with some Château Lafite. Dil then fills his own glass with a nonalcoholic beverage.

"Well, I'm warning you—I fight dirty," Digby says, clinking his glass with Dil Shad's.

Dil apparently finds Digby's remark utterly hilarious; the Persian issues a full-body laugh that leaves him wiping away tears from his eyes. It would seem that the fathers-in-law-to-be have bonded.

Later in the evening, after Digby has not only consumed several glasses of the Lafite, but a few of the second course wine, a Sauvignon Viognier, he leans over to Dil Shad and says, "I hope you don't mind my asking, but we're doing an issue of our magazine about the philosophy of love and sex, and I'm wondering what you can tell me about the relationship between the two in Persian philosophy."

Dil Shad appears affronted. "It is not our custom," he says cryptically.

Digby wisely decides to drop the subject.

It is not until the break before dessert that Digby is finally able to spend a few relatively private moments with his daughter and her betrothed. They both appear aglow with love, possibly also aglow with sex. Sylvia has never looked so unguarded and content. Ahmed has his father's handsome head, except with blue-black hair. Digby wonders if the family is some kind of Persian royalty.

"We are so honored you could come," Ahmed says, shaking Digby's hand.

Digby is so overcome with a strain of gratitude previously unfamiliar to him—thankfulness that this handsome young man has appeared in his daughter's life—that he pulls Ahmed close and wraps his arms around him.

"Dad!" Sylvie laughs. "You are something else."

Indeed, Digby does feel like something else: a normal, happy man thrilled to be at his only child's wedding.

Considering that Phil Weinstein spent upward of $300,000 on the ceremony and reception at the Palo Alto Hills Country Club, the entire bash is surprisingly tasteful. Recognition is paid to the Christian tradition, the Muslim tradition, and to Phil. During the dancing portion of the festivities, Digby sees Sylvie motioning to him; she pantomimes that she wants him to dance with her mother. This is one waltz that Digby would prefer to sit out. It puts him in mind of the Leonard Cohen lyric, "Take this waltz/With its very own breath of brandy and Death." But this, of all evenings, is one to fulfill one's offspring's every desire, so he asks Fanny for the traditional twirl and that they do. Digby strains to make light conversation, but Fanny is as dour and tight-assed as when she had been married to him. As a sign of Digby's new maturity, he does not experience even a scintilla of *schadenfreude* with this observation.

On the flight back, Digby reads selections of *The Lost Love Letters of Héloïse and Abélard* for clues to the medieval conception of a woman's love, but once again panic forces him to cut short his studies. It is Héloïse's uncle's precipitous castration of Abélard that causes Digby to slam his book shut this time.

Only four days after he departed Louden, Digby returns to discover that Associate Dean June MacLane has begat Reuben Jr. The baby had arrived a full week earlier than expected, but was in mint condition, meriting a '9' on the Apgar Scale—very pink, excellent pulse rate, reflexes, muscle tone, and respiration, not to mention the requisite number of fingers and toes. Both Mary and Ada were in attendance. From June's arrival at Copley Hospital in Morristown, Vermont to Reuben's emergence, fewer than five hours elapsed. June took him in her arms for a few moments, then Mary for several minutes. A nurse fed little Reuben with a bottle. On campus later that day, Ada was reportedly seen in a laser-cut minidress handing out cigars.

Reuben Jr. came home the next morning, and mother and child set off for Rockport early the following day, only a few hours before Digby's arrival back in town. He was told that a good number of Mary's parishioners had appeared for her send-off. They applauded when she stepped out of the church door with her baby in her arms.

"Hi. Congratulations!" This seems to be Digby's regular greeting these days.

He has waited a full day before phoning Mary in Rockport. This is not so much out of deference to Mary's busy new life as that it took him a full day to attain a certain lightness of being necessary for this call, to try again to be the one person in Mary's life who does not take everything so damned seriously. Actually, Digby has only reached the perimeter of bearable lightness, but he thinks this is as close as he is going to get.

"Hello, Digby. How was the wedding?" Digby hears some mewls and hiccoughs as a kind of musical ornament under her voice. He pictures Mary cradling little Reuben in one arm as she speaks.

"Very nice, actually," he says. "But what's this? I turn my back and you abscond with your son."

This is not what Digby intended to say. Not even close. In fact, he had repeatedly rehearsed the line, "So, is everything terrific out there?" A cheery, upbeat line, not the guilt-monger-ing downer that came out of his mouth.

"I just needed to start everything new all at one time," Mary says.

"So, is everything terrific out there?" There, he said it.

"Well, hectic and terrific," Mary says.

"I bet. Is there any way I can be helpful?"

"Not right now, Digby. I just have to find a rhythm, you know."

"Of course." Digby is sinking fast. But before his head goes under, he blurts out, "I have some really funny stories to tell you, Mary."

The pathetic last words of a drowning man.

"Hey, I need to warm Ruby's bottle now," Mary says. "Thank you so much for calling, Digby."

Bubble, bubble, gurgle, gurgle.

Remarkably, downcast as Digby is as he hangs up, he remains convinced that he and Mary are meant for one another. One reason for this may be that he detected a faint vibration coming over the phone line from Rockport, a vibe that Mary had tried her best to hide because she believed it was utterly unfair to ask of him. That vibe said, Wait for me to be ready for you, Digby. Please.

CHAPTER **23**

Although Digby has been preoccupied with the concept of 'love' on all fronts of his life, he did not have a clue to what was coming to pass between Attorney Robert Baskerton and the Widow Hastings. He was certainly the last on his staff to realize that Baskerton was wooing Felicia, apparently wooing her with an old fashioned M.O.: sending her bouquets, taking her out to dinners in upscale Burlington restaurants, and—Digby's favorite—sitting across from her in her Victorian salon and reading aloud from Robert Browning and Wilfred Owen. Only a handful of local people were invited to their wedding, which took place a mere four weeks after LeFevre's departure. Digby was not among them.

Digby honestly believes that for Baskerton this is the fulfillment of a long-nurtured dream. It is love, the genuine article—that is, depending on which philosopher of love one happens to be reading. Yet many Louden people now believe that Baskerton is as much an opportunist as the handsome suitor who preceded him. Not long after his wedding, Baskerton incorporated *Cogito* as a for-profit enterprise, naming himself and Felicia as co-executive publishers. Digby received this news in a mass email—apparently Baskerton's grandson had helped the old man buy a computer and set up an email account.

But it is not Baskerton, his bride, or even *Cogito* magazine that preys on Digby's mind this morning; what does there prey is Dr. Aaron Epstein, his former psychotherapist. Epstein had a starring role in Digby's dream last night and, although the

Byzantine plot of the dream is now murky, Digby remembers seeing Epstein's leonine head and tender eyes gazing out at him from his dreamwork television set at one point. Epstein apparently had his own show called, *Just Wondering*. Viewers called in asking him questions about what they should do—with their children, their spouses, their jobs, their lives.

As it happens, Digby still remembers Epstein's office phone number from twenty-odd years ago, not that surprising considering that there was a period in Digby's life when he called Epstein frequently at exactly five minutes to the hour—when the doctor was between sessions—to ask some pressing question like if the doctor thought it would be bad for Digby's self-esteem if he deliberately got himself fired from *Food Stylist* magazine and went on unemployment insurance. ("Yes, it would.")

Digby now dials that number and a woman answers.

"I'm looking for Dr. Aaron Epstein, the therapist," Digby says to her.

"Oh, dear me," the woman says.

"He has an office on Central Park West," Digby says.

"He did. For thirty-eight years."

"And now?"

"And now he doesn't," the woman says.

"Is he—?"

"He's here. In the living room. Watching television in the middle of the morning."

"Do you think I could speak with him?"

"Who is this?"

"Maxwell. Digby Maxwell. I was a patient of Dr. Epstein. I doubt he will remember me."

"Who knows what Aaron remembers?" the woman says. "Wait a minute, Mr. Maxwell."

Digby hears a muffled conference in the background and then the unmistakable voice of Dr. Aaron Epstein.

"Of course, I remember you, Maxwell," he says. "You're the dirty writer."

Yes, indeed; what Aaron Epstein obviously remembers is Digby's *Voice* article about picking up bedmates at his group therapy sessions, the article that marked the end of Digby's tenure as his patient. Clearly, it made a lasting impression on Epstein, albeit a repugnant one. But Digby soldiers on.

"I had a dream about you last night," Digby says.

Epstein laughs. "So you decided to call me up after twenty years to see if I'm still alive."

"Well, that's not the only reason," Digby says. "But it is a good start. Your still being alive, that is."

"Actually, I was sure *you* would be dead by now, Maxwell," Epstein says.

Digby finds Epstein's remark disquieting to say the least, so much so that he feels his pulse rate accelerate into the high stress zone. It occurs to Digby that Epstein is actually trying to induce in him a heart attack—a telephonic, psychokinetic murder as payback for his "Group Sex" piece.

"How did you think I'd croak?" Digby asks.

"I hadn't gotten that far," Epstein says. "Maybe choking on your own spleen."

"Jesus, it was just a dumb article, Doctor!" Digby cries out, his inner child—the one with whom Epstein, two decades earlier, had urged Digby to become reacquainted—bursting forth.

"It wasn't dumb at all," Epstein says. "It was smart and, worse, it was true. I *was* running a dating service. Maybe even a whorehouse. A fucking whore—"

Digby now hears what sounds like a children's scuffle at the other end of the line, the woman who answered the phone clamoring, "Aaron, please!" and "You don't know what you're saying!" A few moments later, Epstein is back on the phone.

"Miriam wants me to tell you that I have a condition," Epstein says calmly. "It's called Giddy Disinhibition Disorder, if you can believe that. GDD in the diagnostic manual. It means I tell the truth. It comes right out of my mouth, unvarnished, *shmutz* and all. I can't stop it. It's a kind of Tourette's syndrome for seniors. They want me to take pills for it, but I don't want to."

"I'm actually glad to hear that," Digby says. "Because that's why I called. I need some truth. The pure stuff."

"About what?"

"You probably don't remember, but you once told me my basic problem was that I didn't take anything seriously enough. My life, everything."

Dr. Epstein starts to laugh, at first softly, but it gradually expands to a wheezy cackle.

"What's so funny?" Digby asks.

"I was full of shit," Epstein manages to say after catching his breath. "It's all a joke, Maxwell. A real whopper. Nothing adds up to anything. Do you hear me?"

With that, either Aaron or Miriam Epstein hangs up the phone.

Chapter 24

Digby Maxwell is strolling through the Louden College campus toting an Uncommon Grounds recyclable paper bag containing a double latte and a corn muffin. The sun is bright, the air crisp and clear. It is final exam time at the college and some students are sitting in groups of two and three under the full-leafed maple trees, books open, pens and notebooks out. It strikes Digby that a calm earnestness now pervades the campus. Is it because of the exams? The proximity of summer vacation and the sentimental farewells that will precede it? Or has a gentle serious-mindedness gradually descended here as a result of President Herker's bizarre, piggyback anagnorisis on the Administration Building patio?

Although he had intended to bring his coffee and snack back to his office as a little pick-me-up before his staff meeting, Digby sits himself down on a quad bench, removes his latte, and takes a few leisurely sips. Aaron Epstein's Giddy Disinhibition Disorder and especially his final bit of unvarnished truth-telling have been knocking about in Digby's mind since their conversation a couple of days ago. Epstein has a 'condition,' according to his wife. What condition would that be—the human one?

And what is Digby's own condition these days? Retrograde Adolescent Infatuation Disorder? Is there a pill for that? If so, does he want to take it? Digby certainly understands why Aaron Epstein does not want to take a pill to cure his condition— because Epstein *is* his condition. Telling the 'shmutzy' truth as he sees it defines who he is at this time, so taking a pill would be tantamount to opting to become a different person. That—becoming a different person—has finally lost its appeal to Digby.

But what about the 'It's all a joke' thing? Digby happens to be somewhat of an expert on jokes, even, he might say, a connoisseur of them: Irish jokes, Jewish jokes, Scandinavian 'Ole and Lena' jokes, even Hindi 'Stupid Sadar' jokes via Asim. He knows their optimum structure, the value of broad-stroke character development and narrative detail in the setups of the best of them. And God knows, Digby can grasp the setup Epstein is referring to in that 'All.' It is the punch line that eludes him.

No, Digby thinks, biting into his corn muffin, it is worse than that. It is his own individual setup that is now absent, what the philosopher Edmund Husserl would call his *Weltanschauung*. The universe, the world, his life—none of them seems all that funny to him these days. He is losing both his cosmic and comic perspectives on himself because he is finding it increasingly difficult to see himself as just another object out there in the cosmos connected to nothing.

The golden couple, Felicia and Robert, are already in Digby's office by the time he returns, but, thankfully, Bonner's old oak chair—*Digby's* old oak chair—remains vacant and awaits him. He is also grateful that he finished his snack and tossed his paper bag before returning. His coffee-and-muffin-for-one would have appeared ungracious.

"I'm afraid no catering this time," Digby says cheerfully as he sits down. He takes out his folder of article ideas and proposed writers for *Cogito*'s 'Love and Sex' number and makes a fine show of studying it. June, Elliot, and Madeleine file in moments later. That is when Bob Baskerton rises with his own file folder in hand. He smiles at Felicia, then individually at each of them before speaking.

"I've got a little business report for us," he begins. "And let me tell you, it's a doozy. As of yesterday at the close of business, we are in our fourth print run of the Heaven Issue, and that's only for newsstand sales. New subscriptions are already up five hundred percent, and we're thinking of sending those new folks the Heaven number free as a little gift, so that'll mean another print run of several thousand copies."

Felicia applauds at this point and Madeleine, God bless her, pipes up with a "Bravo!" Even Digby and June do a few claps before Baskerton continues.

"Those advertising fellas, Saatchi & Saatchi, are beside themselves with enthusiasm," he says.

"Beside *each other*!" Felicia quips.

By golly, the woman has turned into a wit. Digby is not sure this is a good sign.

"For the next issue, they have upped their ad buy to ten full pages and six half pages," Baskerton goes on. "Dewar's Scotch, BMW automobiles, some resort called Canyon Ranch. The kind of stuff our readers like to buy."

Ah yes, our readers, only recently known as consumers of sleaze.

Baskerton finishes up his report by announcing that Cogito, Inc. is making a sizeable, but tax-deductible, gift to Louden College for the express purpose of adding a three-room, high-ceilinged annex to the president's residence. "To give Mr. Herker a little stretching room," Baskerton says, grinning. Baskerton pauses here, apparently expecting a laugh, but if a cute or possibly even naughty *double entendre* was buried in that 'stretching room' phrase, it escapes them all, except, of course, Mrs. Hastings-Baskerton, who titters appreciatively. Digby suspects she heard the line earlier in the day at an informal rehearsal in their breakfast room where she also rehearsed her titter.

"Okay, Digby," Baskerton finishes up. "You take it from here. What kind of magic do you have up your sleeve for the 'Sex' number?"

Digby studies his notes for a moment, then looks up and smiles.

"As usual, I had to do some serious cramming to get up to speed on this one. I'm kind of like these kids you see all over the campus these days cracking their books for the first time a few days before the final exam."

This elicits a laugh only slightly louder than the sound of one hand clapping.

"A lot of people have weighed in on the subject of love," Digby continues. "From Héloïse to Hugh Hefner, from Merleau-Ponty to Madonna, from Blaise Pascal to Candace Bushnell."

All right! Digby is hot, on a tear, his right brain spinning faster than a Dyson vacuum cleaner. Attention is being paid.

"For starters, are there different kinds of love? Is love for a friend different from love for a lover? How about love for a BMW or Dewar's Scotch?"

Digby is not clear what his right brain had in mind with this last bit—perhaps it just threw it in for a laugh, but only Elliot Goldenfield is forthcoming with one. The Baskertons, on the other hand, appear singularly unamused. Digby suspects that his left brain needs to engage in a little giddiness inhibiting.

"Then there is the question of what do love and sex have to do with one another? Let me put that another way—how can you tell if you really are in love or you just have a libidinal itch?"

Bob Baskerton likes this one, even if Digby does detect some impatience creeping onto his craggy brow.

"And then, of course, there is the question of defining love," Digby goes on. Here, he suddenly breaks into song with the line, " 'When the stars make you drool just like a pasta fazool, that's amore.' . . . Now does *that* definition do the trick?"

It is at this point that the uneasy glances and skeptical squints begin. They come at him from all corners of the office. It would seem impossible to ignore them. Yet Digby blithely does.

"I mean, is Dean Martin any less an authority on 'amore' than old Aristotle? Our good friend Rostislav Demidov would say that love denotes no more than a range and pattern of squirts in our endocrine system. But where do you go from there? Come to think of it, where did Rosti go from there once he started to drool like a pasta fazool? Back to Moscow with his heart bleeding in his hands—that's where he went."

Digby would not deny that there was a certain amount of bitterness in his tone in this last line, but he will always contend that it was out of his personal control.

Madeleine's uneasy glance morphs into a sneer of contempt, mirroring her emotional transition from concern for Digby's mental stability to wishing that he would drop dead on the spot.

Digby sees her brace her hands against the arms of her chair as if about to propel herself up and at him. This must be it—the fulfillment of Aaron Epstein's prophecy. Digby's untimely demise, choked by Madeleine acting as a surrogate for his own spleen. Thankfully, June places a calming hand on Madeleine's shoulder and she remains seated.

Digby takes a deep breath. He reopens his folder and closes it again. He blinks involuntarily for several seconds. His spinning head slows like a wobbly top returning to stasis. And then he begins again.

It is I who speaks.

"I need to tell you that love is serious stuff. In fact, it is the only reliable thing anybody can come up with to give meaning to life. It is, as they say, what makes the world go 'round. And that is why I am assigning articles to some very bright and thoughtful people. People like Professor Arthur McRitchie of Purdue University, a disciple of the existentialist Rollo May who saw love as essential to human survival. Professor McRitchie has some fascinating ideas on how loving is a transcendent act, a way of merging our I-ness with a profound Thou-ness. I've also tapped Professor Edith Pelati, a Harvard classicist who has developed a fascinating deconstruction of the term 'Eros' in the early Platonic dialogues. She has some dazzling insights into how loving the form of beauty is the basis of what she calls our 'aesthetic libido.' And I am particularly happy to report that Professor Avi Aaronson, a scholar at Hebrew Theological Seminary, will contribute a chapter from the volume he has been working on for twenty-some years on the concept of uncompromising love in the Old Testament. Aaronson has some unusual insights into the relationship between the biblical concept of fear of the otherness and the biblical concept of love of the otherness."

Digby gazes out upon his audience. With the exception of Goldenfield who is applauding avidly, they are making eye contact with the floor, sounding a distant bell in Digby's memory. After a silence of staggering dimensions, Baskerton clears his throat.

"Saatchi & Saatchi—" he begins, but then falls silent again.

Only minutes later, everyone picks up and departs, leaving Digby alone in his office overlooking the tulip garden. He feels remarkably at peace.

I am here now.

EPILOGUE

I am sitting in my office at the *Gloucester Times* where I have just finished writing a survey of open-to-the-public musical events coming up on the Cape Ann waterfront. I may have squandered more ink than I should have on Old Cold Tater, a bluegrass band that will be playing tonight on the bandstand at Rockport's Back Beach, but I listened to them practice this afternoon and these guys deserve to be heard. I have an inkling that Old Cold Tater just might make it to Boston in the coming year.

I check my watch—it is just past five, so I call it a day. Mary has to correct papers tonight, so I'll grab supper at Captain Carlo's and then head back to my apartment on Smith's Cove and read some more Thoreau. I only see Mary and little Ruby when she has the time. On these occasions, the three of us have dinner in her kitchen and afterward I put her son to bed, singing him my original lullaby, "Ruby is Such a Little Snooby." It has proved to be suitably soporific. Afterward, Mary and I sit on the couch in her little living room. We talk and laugh and kiss one another tenderly.

I am patiently awaiting my final goofy blessing—my lucky, if tricky, ending.